WHY WOULD YOU LEAD ME ON?

T. COLLINS

authorHOUSE®

AuthorHouse™
1663 Liberty Drive
Bloomington, IN 47403
www.authorhouse.com
Phone: 833-262-8899

This is a work of fiction. All of the characters, names, incidents, organizations, and dialogue
in this novel are either the products of the author's imagination or are used fictitiously.

Published by AuthorHouse   07/09/2021

ISBN: 978-1-6655-3163-4 (sc)
ISBN: 978-1-6655-3164-1 (hc)
ISBN: 978-1-6655-3167-2 (e)

Print information available on the last page.

This book is printed on acid-free paper.

IT'S COLD AS HELL OUTSIDE. I HAVE TO SIT HERE AND WAIT FOR THIS damn bus. I looked at that schedule before I came outside. The bus said it would be here at 7:00 pm. Where the fuck is this bus? It's 7:30 pm now. I'm going to be late for work. Here I am sitting, in this damn cold, and I wish I had a car. Then again, my ass will not drive for shit.

Here goes this guy walking. I hope he does not speak to me. I am not in the mood for this thirsty shit tonight. Guys see women at night waiting for a bus, and they always talk to you. I am so over it. I just want to get my bread and move on.

A guy started walking towards her. He had on sweatpants and a sweatshirt. His name is Xavier. He looked at Cecilia as if he didn't even notice her.

Thank god I thought he was going to be annoying and try and talk to me. A couple of days later, she saw this same guy again.

He was coming from the store, and there she was, alone, waiting for the bus again.

"Hey, I don't want to bother you, but uhm, never mind."

Cecilia thought that it was kind of odd that he just came up and said that.

"Excuse me, what's up."

"Honestly, I had everything I wanted to say to you, but you make me kind of nervous. I don't want to say the wrong words.

Cecilia smiled. She never heard a guy use this approach before.

"Thank you," she said with a smile.

"Your eyes are unique, and that smile you have is impressive. Has anyone told you that you have the eyes of an angel?

Cecilia didn't notice her bus was coming. The bus had gone past her. Once Cecilia notices her bus was gone, she became angry. He sees how angry she became from the glare in her eyes.

"I needed that bus to get to work."

"I am sorry, I didn't mean it. I just wanted to talk to you. Listen, I have a car. I can drive you where you need to go."

"I can't do that. I barely know you."

"Well, I am not crazy. I live right around the corner, and my kids live with me."

"I am sorry, thank you. I rather get on the bus. It's not your fault."

I glance at his face. The stare that I gave him was so intense he could see my annoyance without saying a word.

Another bus was going to be coming soon. Cecilia did not want to take that chance of getting into a stranger's car. It was bad enough she was talking to him.

"I understand. I feel bad. Would you like me to wait with you for the next bus?"

"No"

"Damn, okay, I guess I will go home. Be safe."

Cecilia was irritated even more. She could not afford to be late for her job. It was two hours away from Philadelphia on the bus. The last bus that she needs to catch after the first bus from home leaves at 11 pm.

Oh, my fucking goodness, I miss my bus. I am not trying to be late for work. I am on my second strike with this job.

Cecilia loved to work. She seems to have everything for herself as long as she didn't get involved with men. Cecilia does not know how to focus when she is in a relationship.

Cecilia is forty years old and could pass for a teenager or her early twenties.

Cecilia has a daughter named Lyrica Harris. Lyrica is a songwriter a poet, and the way she sings will make you cry tears of joy.

Lyrica stayed working out daily, and she is a true vegan. She didn't believe in no meat. Everything had to be plant-based.

Let me check to see when this next bus comes. Cecilia used her phone to google search and checked to see when the next bus came. The time showed the next bus arrives at 9:00 p.m. Cecilia was furious, so she called a uber.

I can't believe I have to spend more money to get the fuck to work. The uber came in ten minutes for Cecilia. The only problem is she had to share the ride with someone else. The customer was intoxicated. He kept trying to talk to her and get her phone number. Cecilia was getting very annoyed.

Man, this cannot be life. Please just let me get to work safely and in peace!

Cecilia arrived to work, running to the time clock.

"Hey everyone!" said Cecilia

Cecilia was in the breakroom with her co-workers. She had been at her job for five years, working overnight. She works at a nursing home. Cecilia stayed to herself in her neighborhood. However, when she went to work, she was very social.

Xavier had been living in the West oak lane section for about seven years. He had his own house, and he drove a Mercedes-Benz. He took care of his kids by himself.

Xavier was home thinking about Cecilia while watching television. He knew he wanted to see her again. He felt like it was going to be impossible now.

The next day came. Cecilia decided to wait for the bus a little earlier. She did not want to run into the guy from yesterday, and she tried to get to work on time.

It worked out well for her for a while. She would leave out at the same time every day. Until one day she saw him.

Xavier walked over towards her.

"Hi …How are you? My name is Xavier." He said

Cecilia glance at him. She notices his eyes, his physique, his voice, the waves in his hair, his tattoos, and she damn near wanted to melt.

"Hi Xavier…" she said, pausing to pronounce his name correctly

"Yeah, I'm sorry for having you missed your bus the other day. I can give you a ride to work if you like."

"That sounds tempting, but my job is far, and I don't even know you. I told you that before. Cecilia replied

"Hey, it's cool. Can I get your number instead?" said Xavier

"Well, I mean, you're cute and all, but I'm not trying to be talking to nobody right now. I'm trying to stay to myself. I got myself married to the money." said Cecilia

"Give me a break. I want to show you something different," said Xavier

"Ok, I guess," she said, with a smile

"Damn, you have some pretty ass white teeth. I love your smile," Xavier said

Xavier had a thing for women who kept their self up and had all of their teeth. He liked Cecilia at first glance. He felt the vibe that she had her head on straight.

Cecilia gave him her number. He had a wristwatch, and he put her number in his wristwatch.

"Wait! What is that?"? said Cecilia,

You ain't never seen a phone with a wristwatch to it. I can use my watch to make phone calls and text and do everything else." Said, Xavier

"Oh, that's hot. How old are you, Xavier?"

Cecilia started to chuckled

"Why you laugh? I'm thirty-two years old," said Xavier

"I'm forty years old. I am laughing because I did not notice how fine you were until now," said Cecilia

"Thank you. Damn, you look young as shit! Let me see some ID. You look like a baby," said Xavier

Cecilia pulled out her wallet, and she showed Xavier her ID.

"Damn, you look good as hell for your age! That smile girl it lights up the whole room," said Xavier

"Thank you. My bus coming, so look, I am going to hit you up later," said Cecilia

"My offer still on the table to take you to work," said Xavier

"Naw, I'm cool," said Cecilia

Cecilia got on that bus happy.

I could of let him give me a ride to one of the buses. I know this is a long ride, though. He could be some stalker, too, and come up to my job one day being reckless. It has happened to me before. I don't need to make that mistake again. I know what I will do. I will just text him.

Soon as Cecilia was about to text Xavier. He had called her first.

"Hey, what's up, Cee- Cee. I hope you don't mind me calling you that." said Xavier

"Oh no, you're cool. I don't mind you calling me that. No one has called me that since I was younger. I was just about to text you, and you called me first." Said Cecilia

"Oh, ok. Damn, you are so attractive. Why are you single?" said Xavier

"I caught my ex cheating while I was scrolling through the pages on Facebook. He had got locked up, and this gorilla-looking bitch was all happy to say that he was with her in the comments. He told me he was in jail with his first phone call. I broke up with him while he was in jail. When he got out, he married her"

"Oh damn, that's, fuck up. Well, listen, my baby mother and me, we are separated right now. However, I am not going to hold you, but I still fuck her." said Xavier

"Damn, that's a little bold." Said, Cecilia

"Naw, I'm just keeping it real with you. That's giving you a choice to deal with me while I'm with my baby mom. You women always say guys never give you all a choice. So, don't do that," said Xavier

"No, that's what's up. I like it. Besides, you and I are going to to be friends." said Cecilia

"Cool, now that we got that understanding, what are you looking for," said Xavier

"I'm not looking for nothing but companionship, no strings attached. However, if you decide you will be with your baby mom exclusively or someone else permanently, I am out. I cannot stay around for that. said, Cecilia

"Oh, that's cool. I like that. So what do you like to do." said Xavier

"I don't do too much. I work and try and get money the best way I can legally. My daughter is in college, so I don't have no one to take care of besides myself," said Cecilia

"Oh, ok, so you into the movies or anything."

"Hell yeah! I want to see the new" Pac" movie."

"Oh, I saw it. I don't mind seeing it again. It was good."

"Cool we out then," said Cecilia

"Alright, listen, I have some things I have to take care of, so I'm going hit you back. But, you have a nice night at work," Said Xavier

"Thank you. Have a nice day as well," Said Cecilia

Man, he sounds so good over the phone. It's a shame that he got a situation, and it seems like all these men do. That's why I'm single now.

When Cecilia arrived at work, she was so happy that she gave out good customer service. She never spoke with her patients in years.

Soon as the morning came, she noticed Xavier had been trying to call her. Cecilia had her phone on silent since she was at work. She decided to call him

"Hey, Xavier, this is Cecilia. I notice you called me. What's up?" asked Cecilia

"Hey yeah. Are you off work yet? Question Xavier

"Yeah, I'm about to go home." Said Cecilia

"Oh, you want to go get breakfast," said Xavier

"I mean sure, but I won't arrive in Philly until 8:30 a.m or 9'oclock in the morning," said Cecilia,

"Oh, that's cool. When you get to the Chestnut hill loop, let me know. I can meet you up there. I am leaving now." said Xavier

"Ok, where are we going to eat," said Cecilia

"We can eat at IHOP if you want," said Xavier

"Ok. thanks. I would love that," said Cecilia with excitement

Cecilia was feeling like a teenager all over again. The love she was feeling was making her happy. She was anticipating how this would lead.

"Look at you, smiling Cecilia," said Camila

Camila was Cecilia's coworker.

"Who that in the background?" asks Xavier

"My coworker Camila," said Cecilia

"Alright, listen, I will meet you up at the Chestnut Hill Loop Xavier. I will talk to you when I see you later then," said Xavier

"Okay, see you soon," said Cecilia

Cecilia hung up the phone.

"Ok, Cecilia, what's good. Who got you smiling like this? He got you looking like a high school girl." said Camila

"Oh, girl, it's some young boy I met. He lives around my way. I don't usually talk to guys around my way, though." said Cecilia

"Oh, that's cool. Just be careful about talking to guys around your way. That's a little bit too close to home. You know when drama sparks, it will be at your doorstep, so be safe." said Camila

"I should be fine. Xavier let me know how things are, so I'm cool," said Cecilia

"Alright, just don't get caught up, boo, Friends with benefits are cool. However, when a guy says they are still fucking their baby mom, it sometimes means a potential to them getting back together. Nine times of ten their not using a condom. So you can get an std or worse," said Camila

"Girl, I am fine, trust me," said Cecilia

"I am sure you are fine. I think you should know your worth. Xavier is not the one you need in your life. It would help if you searched for something better.

"I have to go. I see my bus."

"Okay."

Cecilia saw her bus coming from around the corner. She ran as quickly as she could. The long bus ride was making her fall asleep on the bus. Xavier called her six times, but she could not hear her phone ring, not one time. Pandora's music played in her ear, and the heat from the bus had put her to sleep.

Finally, she jumped up to see if she was about to miss her stop. She woke up in just the nick of time. She had two more stops. She looked at her phone cause she was just about to call Xavier. That's when she noticed he called her six times. So, she promptly called him back.

"Hey, my bad, I missed your call. I fell asleep on the bus. It's hard-working overnight," said Cecilia

"Oh no, I was calling to see if you needed something. I'm here at the Chestnut Hill Loop. I have a black car. I'm in from of some gas station, and there's a daycare down the street you can't miss me." said Xavier

It was the end of the line for her stop. Cecilia knew what gas station he was talking about because the gas station was across the street. As soon as you get off the bus, you would see it. She felt drained, but she wanted to eat breakfast after a long day at work.

"I'm on my way. I'm getting off the bus now, do you see me" said Cecilia

"Yes, I see you," said Xavier

He started flashing his headlights. So Cecilia could see precisely where he is parked. Cecilia looked around for a black car to be parked. There he was, sitting in the car waiting for her.

Cecilia was tired, and her body was aching. She did not want to give up on a chance to be treated for breakfast. As soon she got in the car, you could notice the pain she felt.

"Hey Xavier," said Cecilia

Cecilia reached for the door to open it, and she hopped inside the car.

Damn, I never noticed how good he looked until now. His eyes were hypnotizing me. I can't believe he was this fine. All the tattoos he had on his body turned me on even more. His body looks so good I want to taste him until he tells me to stop.

He had the heat nicely flowing in the car. The temperature was not too powerful.

I leaned over and hugged him.

"What was that for? he asked with a chuckled

"I'm just happy to see you. We met with a little of a rough start. But, I am learning that you are an okay dude."

"Thank you. You look tired as shit. How was work, though?"

"I am tired. I work overnight, so my body is sore. "

"I don't know how you do this. I would be tired as shit."

"I do get a little tired sometimes. Can you turn on the radio?"

"Sure, what station you want or should I say what type of music do you want to hear"

"I don't know. Put on some old-school shit."

Xavier took one look at Cecilia, and her eyes seem to glimmer in the sunlight. It turned him on to see how attractive her eyes were.

"Do you know you have some pretty eyes, girl?

"No, People tell me that I have bedroom eyes," said Cecilia

Xavier turned on the radio to an old-school radio station.

Cecilia kept looking around in his car. She was so intrigued by his car.

All of a sudden, Cecilia's song came on the radio. It was called "Am I dreaming" by Ol Skool featuring Xscape, and Keith Sweat

"Oh my, that's my song! I haven't heard this song in years."

"Yeah, that is a classic. Xscape was just on the Bet awards. They had a reunion."

"Wait, you don't have any keys in the car! How the hell are you driving this car?" said Cecilia

"It's keyless. I don't need a key to drive. I just press this button to start the engine up. Since you just got off work, I will put on the massage feature." said Xavier

Xavier hit the massage feature of his car. Cecilia felt the pulsing vibes go through her body.

"Damn, I never saw anything like that before! This feels good as fuck," said Cecilia

Xavier smiled at her.

"So do you drink or smoke," asked Xavier

"Well, I'm a drinker. I don't smoke at all," said Cecilia

"Oh, ok, that's good. You will be smoking soon with me," said Xavier

Xavier is a lady's man. He knew she would be doing things she wouldn't normally do. Xavier had his eyes set on her. He knew soon he would get her. He just was trying to figure out what her angle was.

He wanted to know in detail about her. He found her so unique and attractive.

The right songs were coming on the radio. Cecilia was smiling and dancing in the chair. Then she suddenly fell asleep. The massage from the chair helped her go to sleep even more.

Xavier didn't want to wake her up by talking until they had arrived at the IHOP.

Cecilia looked so sweet and seductive while she was sleeping in the chair.

Xavier glanced over a couple of times, wanting to kiss her. She looked so relaxed. Cecilia didn't even know she was sleeping.

Until Xavier gently woke her up to let her know they had arrived at the local IHOP not too far from them.

"Oh my god, we are here. I didn't realize I fell asleep. I hope I was not snoring." said Cecilia

Cecilia pulled the sun visor from the car down to look into the mirror. She had examined her face to make sure she looked presentable. She began to get a dove wipe out of her purse and wiped her face.

"No, you were good. You looked cute just laying there in the car," said Xavier.

Cecilia smiled. She felt comfortable that he reassured her that he could be a gentleman.

They both got out of the car at the same time. She grabbed her purse and shut the door. Xavier uses his car remote to lock the doors. The alarm sound went off for about three seconds.

Cecilia felt very happy. They walked inside the restaurant, and it didn't seem to be too crowded in there. They were seated right away. Xavier had chosen for them to have a booth. He wanted to be able to talk to her and give her direct eye contact.

The waitress had brought the menus. She had announced her name was Tamika, and she would be their server for the day. Cecilia glanced over the menu.

"Order whatever you want," said Xavier

Cecilia smiled, and she politely said, "Thank you." Then, she looked at him and started looking at the menu again.

The waitress came back in five minutes and asked them were they ready to order. They both were ready, so they placed their orders.

"I want to get an order of hotcakes, sausages, and scrambled eggs with cheese," said Cecilia

"Okay, sir, and what would you like to have?" asked the waitress

"Steak omelet with an order of pancakes."

"Okay would you like anything to drink." asked the waitress

"Yeah, I want a coffee," said Cecilia

"Oh, you can give me an orange juice," said Xavier

"Uhm can I get a glass of ice water with lemon as well," said Cecilia

"Sure," said the waitress

The waitress wrote down their orders. She took the menus off the table. She let them know she would be right back with their food.

As they were waiting for their food, Cecilia and Xavier began talking.

11

Xavier was listening, but his mind was thinking about all the positions he could put her in. Unbeknownst to her, Xavier was a professional in the bedroom.

Cecilia did not know that she was about to get herself into a crazy situation. All she knew was she needed to get out. Cecilia got tired of telling guys no. She wanted to be with someone who was going to be a companion. Cecilia was not seeing anyone. She just was not ready to commit to anyone. Every guy was the wrong guy. So she decided to leave men alone for a while. Cecilia put her focus into working in hopes that she would never have to deal with men again.

Life became more manageable for her. She didn't see the need to go out or drink anymore. Cecilia had back-to-back breakups. So she didn't see herself getting involved with anyone. She didn't see it for at least a while.

The food came after about half an hour. Cecilia was glad that the food came because she was starving.

The coffee was fresh and, how she requested it.

Xavier was hungry as well.

"This is the perfect omelet. So can you cook" asked Xavier

"Yeah, I went to school to become a Chef, and I took up some other trades along the way. My specialty is really in baking. I bake on the side as a side hustle. I can bake anything," said Cecilia

Cecilia took out her phone, and she showed him all the photos she had. She couldn't wait to show off her baking skills to him.

Xavier was impressed. He was just hoping she was not lying. He had a lot of women in his past lying, saying they can cook. Then they would get in the kitchen and damn near burn the house down. Women would always try to impress him. He is just used to it.

Xavier and Cecilia were at the table, discussing their likes and dislikes. She was please to know he had it going on for someone his age. Usually, guys around his age were still living with their mom. She met the type of guys who live with their girlfriends, sold drugs, lied, abusive, and were up to no good. She still wanted to be careful with him because he was too good to be true.

Xavier was a big spender, and He could afford to spend money like that. He was making over $40.00 an hour at his job. Cecilia had a lot going on with him. He left the waitress with a $10 tip.

Cecilia was impressed with him. She couldn't believe what a charmer he was. They walked over to the car. He opened the door for her. Then she slid over to open the driver-side door for him.

"Thanks, CeCe. So, tell me, why are you single?"

Xavier started locking the door with the remote from the car keys. He sat down once he got in the car, and he put on his seat belt. Then he pressed the start engine button inside his vehicle.

"I am single because I don't settle anymore. Soon as I see bull shit, I'm out. I don't care how cute a guy is, his sex game, how much money he has, or every female wanting him. I need someone to make me feel good and building as a team. I don't deal with fake. I want to be friends first with a guy. In my past, I always allowed myself to get forced into a relationship. It never ends well because I would do it to make the guy happy knowing damn well I just wanted to be his friend first." said Cecilia

Xavier looked at her and nodded his head in agreement. He admired the fact she was an older woman and intelligent.

"I'm single, but I still fuck my baby mom sometimes. I don't see myself going back to her because we always have our issues with different things. I like being single. I don't like to feel tied down. Relationships are demanding." said Xavier

"Yeah, that's about right. I admire your honesty. I don't know if you remember, but you told me about you and your baby mother already. Remember you said some guys lie about the shit they do. It's a turn-off for me anyway. I rather a guy tell me the truth and let me decide what I am going to deal with." said Cecilia

Where do you live? So I can put it in the GPS real quick." said Xavier

Cecilia gave him her address, and he typed it in the device.

"What are you doing later?" I want to see you again." said Xavier

"I have to work tonight. I might have to see you another time. I got to go home and get some sleep." said Cecilia

"Oh damn, that's right, you got that overnight shift. I don't know how you do it seriously those hours I need to sleep or party."

"Yeah, I chose these hours, so I don't get caught up in no relationships."

"Alright, I will just text you then."

Damn, for the first time in a long time, I felt good. It felt good to get out; I felt at peace. I felt like Xavier was my king, and I was his queen.

It was like I was in a trance from him. He looks so sexy; his walk, his talk, and his body. I could lick him from head to toe. I do know if it's because I have not been with a man in a while. Maybe it's his charm. It's still early, and I do not want to jinx shit. I mean, it's just material shit he displayed to me. I do not even know if all this shit is his.

They were getting closer to the house. Xavier noticed she didn't live too far away from him.

"Damn, we are getting close to my house," said Cecilia

"Yeah, we live right down the street from each other. I don't usually date girls that live around my way. It's because when they get a little part of me, they act a little crazy. You seem mature, plus your older, so I don't think you will act like that."

Cecilia just looked at him. She didn't know what to say in response to that. She was just happy to be home.

They had finally arrived at her door. Cecilia couldn't wait to get into her house. Xavier waited for her to open the door, and then he drove off.

Cecilia went upstairs to her bathroom to soak in her drop-down jacuzzi tub. She turned on the water and the radio

Meanwhile, Xavier was at home drinking. He was also thinking of his next move with Cecilia. He was starting to like her.

Xavier decided he wanted to watch a little television. So he started flipping the channels to see what he could watch on television. He ended up falling to sleep.

After Cecilia finished soaking in the tub, she had dried herself off, oiled her body down, put on her deodorant, set her alarm clock, put on her chemise nightgown, and then went to bed.

Hours later, Cecilia's alarm had gone off. She did not want to get up. However, she knew she needed that money. So she made herself get up. She got into her work clothes, ran downstairs, locked her doors, and walked towards the bus.

There he was, waiting for her at the bus stop. Her eyes were bright like a Christmas tree. He walked over to her, and he hugged her.

The hug felt so warm. It was what Cecilia needed. He had a firm grip, so she felt the tingling sensation going through her body.

"I didn't know you were going to be here," said Cecilia

'I know," he said

"Thank you for showing up," said Cecilia

"You're welcome," he said with a smile

He waited with her until her bus came. Cecilia's bus finally arrived, and she got on the bus. She paid her fare and then sat down in her seat. As the bus was moving by, she waved to Xavier, and he waved back.

He smiled at her showing his amazingly bright teeth.

So when Cecilia got to work, she was happy. She saw her co-worker Camila. She always talked to her when she came to work. Camila and Cecilia became cool overnight.

Cecilia walked over to Camila. She couldn't wait to tell her more about Xavier.

"Camila girl, I have to tell you something," said Cecilia

Camila knew Cecilia's story was about to be juicy. She could tell because of the glow she had on her face.

"So, I met this guy name Xavier. You remember I told you about him. Girl, he looks so fucking good." said Cecilia

"Yeah, I remember you telling me about the boy. I thought you said you were leaving guys along for a while," said Camila

"Oh, I think he's different, though. He gave me that glow I have been missing, girl. Plus, he is not trying to rush me into a relationship like the other guys try to do."

Cecilia was delighted Xavier didn't do much, but she felt he would make her happy in her heart.

"Alright, just don't get caught up. You know me, and you are just similar when it comes down to these men. Plus, you said Xavier lives around your way."

Camila became cool with Cecilia when she first came there to the nursing home. Cecilia was fresh out of nursing school. Camila showed her the ropes. She was nervous when she first started working at the nursing home. Camila helped her along the way.

As Cecilia was telling Camila about Xavier, her cell phone rang. She didn't know who it was calling her at first. She took one look at her phone's caller ID and saw it was Xavier.

"Hold up, girl! That's him," said Cecilia

Cecilia started smiling. She was so excited just to talk to him.

"Oh my god, he got you opened," said Camila

"Shut up, girl!" said Cecilia in a joking way

Cecilia answered the call and walked away.

"Hello"

"Hey CeCe, how you doing so far."

"I'm good. I'm at work right now, though."

"Alright, do you want me to call you back?"

"Naw, I'm good. I can talk on the phone. I work overnight, so I don't have to hide my phone. I have earbuds in my ear. They don't pay too much attention to us. So long as we are working, they don't care."

"Oh well, listen, so I want to take you out again. I was thinking we go to the movies and maybe go out to eat."

"Cool, you remember me saying I want to see that new Pac movie," said Cecilia

"I remember, silly. That's where I was going to take you. You forgot we had this conversation. I told you that I had seen it, and I don't mind seeing it again." said Xavier

"Oh yeah, my bad. I have a lot of things on my mind."

"Cool, so when is the next time you have free."

"It will probably be in about a week cause I am trying to catch up on my bills, so I have been doing doubles."

"Oh, ok, I understand. Well, just let me know."

"Wait, I mean, I can meet up with you this Saturday. I was going to ask if I can come into work, but I can chill with you."

"Cool, so what kind of liquor do you like."

"I like Ciroc Peach, or some flavored vodka, maybe even some 99 banana. What do you like?"

"I like Tequila. "

"Oh, I can't drink that shit," said Cecilia as she giggled a little

"Why? It's just liquor."

"Tequila for me means to kill you. I'm good. I woke up on my bathroom floor with no clothes on and vomited all night. I ate something, so I don't care what nobody says about eating before you drink." said Cecilia

"Oh, alright. So, what do you do at work" asked Xavier as he laughed a little

He started thinking about the wild nights when he would drink. Tequila didn't mess with him like that. Xavier could party all night long and be able to get up for work at 6 am. He drinks every night. When it came to women, his goal was to turn them out. He would use them to see how much he could get out of them.

Xavier wanted someone, but his ego would set in. The challenge of the woman playing hard to get would turn him on. Especially if she had the body, the brains, and she carried her own. Xavier respected women who kept a clean house, and he loved when a woman dressed in red. It was something about when a woman wore red and smelled good had him melt like butter.

"I am an RN. I give meds to my patients and some other things too. I work in Flourtown, PA."

"That's pretty far."

"Yeah, I work far to keep away from people in my neighborhood. I love to go to new places. People don't just pop up at your jobs if it's far"

"True," said Xavier

The real reason Cecilia worked far out was that she had an ex from hell. He made her detest all men for a while. John would unexpectedly come up to her job, high off cocaine, angel dust, and embarrassed her place of employment. When he showed up, he would call her bitches and tell people she was nasty and unfit to be a mother. He would also cheat on her and make her feel like she was less of a woman.

When Cecilia found out he was on drugs and cheating on her, she tried to end it. But he didn't want that. She had to get a restraining order. He had someone else pregnant but still wanted to be with her. She wasn't trying to put up with that.

John was not like that when she met him. In her eyes, he could do no wrong. People kept telling her he was cheating. Cecilia was hooked on him because of his sex. John slowly moved his son into her house. He had her watching his son while he would go out and cheat on her with other women. When Cecilia found out, she started reading magazines on Poly relationships.

Cecilia thought if she opened the door to having threesomes, maybe he would stay home. But, on the other hand, Cecilia only wanted to do it because it worked out for her girlfriends, so she thought it would work for her.

One day she came home, there was a condom on her bed. She confronted him, and he lied and said he was just playing a joke on her. Cecilia did not believe it. She told him to get out of her house. However, he would not leave her home. Instead, he pushed her to the ground. A neighbor heard her screaming, came into the house, dragged him out of the house, and beat him up.

After this incident, she realized giving him a threesome would not help the relationship. On the contrary, it would make things worse. She noticed he was on drugs after the big break-up. He made her life a living hell. John was trying to ruin her; that is why he started coming up to her job. He was embarrassed the neighbors came in and fought him.

Eventually, she resigned from her job working at the bank. Instead, she went to school for nursing and found a job at the nursing home.

She still had her trust issues with men. Cecilia has dealt with so much she didn't even trust herself anymore with men. She felt the littlest thing would either make her cheat or break up with them.

Years later, John had got married to another woman. However, Cecilia never forgave him, and she moved her and her daughter to west oak lane.

West oak lane is a section of Philadelphia. Cecilia was living in the northeast area of Philadelphia.

"Hey, well, listen, I'm going to talk to you later, Xavier, so I can get started on this work I have to do."

"Oh, ok. So listen, the day we go out, I probably get us a bottle while we shoot out to the movies."

"Cool! That sounds nice. I will talk to you later."

"Alright, sweety, talk to you later."

Cecilia pushes the end button on her cellular phone to hang up the phone. Now she knows she was not supposed to be with Xavier, but she was catching feelings. She couldn't even hide it.

Meanwhile, Xavier was at home. He was expecting his baby mom to come over to the house. She would come over to the house sometimes and spend the night. His baby mom was a little on the chunky side. Her name is Ciara, but her nickname is CeCe.

19

Ciara is a manager at her hair salon in the Frankford section of Philadelphia. She has four children, and only one of those children is by Xavier. Ciara's goal was to have a chain of hair salons. The downfall of her success was worrying about Xavier. She wanted to do everything for Xavier. However, she was losing her mind trying to satisfy him.

Xavier tries to do right for the females he meets. However, when he sees any sign of weakness towards them, he takes advantage. Xavier does know what he wants from the women. He needs the woman to be strong, secure, family-orientated, a freak in the bedroom, and a lady in the streets. At the same time, he is testing these women to replace his baby mom.

He likes the things his baby mom does, such as cooking, cleaning, and putting the order in the house with the kids. He doesn't want her insecurities. Ciara was constantly worrying about her weight or her stomach.

Sometimes he tests the women he meets for the comfort he is missing, the sex, and the conversation. That was important to him.

Xavier is about 6'1 and 200 pounds with a solid built. Ciara loved that about him she wanted to be his wife someday.

Ciara's nagging about being an Instagram model was getting on his nerves. He loves how she looks in his eyes. He does know how to be faithful to her. Xavier wants to settle down with her. Ciara does not trust him, so he decided to call off the relationship.

The next day had come, and Cecilia could not stop thinking of Xavier.

She talked about him so much that some of her co-workers were getting tired of hearing it. Some of the other co-workers were loving the stories, but they wanted her to be careful.

Everyone wanted her to be careful because they knew about the risks she would be taking with her heart.

Xavier loves Ciara, but he's not ready for her. He tries to let her go, but he's always drawn back to her. Xavier doesn't want to hurt her. That's why he always tries to break up with her before he cheats. Sometimes he cheats while he is with her because she won't let him go. He will tell her over and over that they need counseling to make things right.

Ciara has a house with her best friend, Lisa. She was at home preparing herself to get ready to meet up with Xavier. She wanted to make sure she smelled good.

Xavier decided to call Cecilia. Cecilia saw her phone ringing. She answered the phone, sounding overly excited to talk to him.

"Xavier," said Cecilia smiling so hard as if he could see her.

"Well, you sound happy. "

"I am because you are making me happy I haven't felt this way in a while."

"Oh, that's a good thing," said Xavier with a chuckle.

"I would love to talk to you, but I have to get to work."

"Oh, ok, it's cool, just call me when you can."

"Alright, cool."

As Xavier ended the call, he heard his door open up. He walked downstairs he saw it was Ciara.

She looked at him and smiled.

Xavier jogged down the steps, walked over to her, and hugged her. Her scent had him so intoxicated. He began to kiss her neck.

Ciara was enjoying every moment of his touch. She began to lick her lips. The way she licked her lips turned him on. He gave her a kiss that instantly made her yearn for more. He took off her coat. She was naked underneath that jacket.

The way Ciara's body looked to him just made him feel hypnotize. He was mad that she had low self-esteem and wanted to be an Instagram model.

Xavier became excited, and he gently picked Ciara up. He carried her over to the black leather sofa and laid her down. There she was, rested on the couch. She was anticipating his touch, his warmth, and for him to taste her.

Men would tell Ciara how beautiful she is all the time. Those words meant nothing to her. She wanted to hear them from Xavier. She wanted him to mean it when he said it to her. She loved Xavier more than she loved herself.

"Hold on, don't move. I will be right back," said Xavier

Xavier jogged upstairs, and he grabbed a bottle of baby oil. He came back downstairs, and he saw her still sitting in the same position she was in from before. Xavier walked over to her and gently started pouring the baby oil over her body. Then he sat down next to her. He began to massage the oil all over her body.

The massage had felt good after a long day of work.

Xavier spread her legs apart, and he began to lick every part of her vagina slowly. Then he focuses on her clitoris. She started to become moist, and her legs started shaking. Ciara grabbed his head because the pleasure was getting too intense. She let out a couple of soft moans. At the same time, her eyes felt as if they were rolling to the back of her head.

Xavier was getting aroused with every movement of her soft skin. The perfume she had on smelled so good. She didn't have on a lot like most girls that he dealt with in the past. He was ready to place his penis inside her. She kept holding him down. She grabbed the pillow from the sofa, held it tight, and started moaning louder. Xavier began to lick a little faster, and Ciara exploded in his mouth.

Her body was limp and stiff as aboard. She couldn't move. She felt as if she was in a trance. Xavier slowly took his pajama pants off, gradually places his penis inside of her, and she took a deep breath and exhaled.

"Yessssssss," said Ciara as she moaned

Xavier was well-endowed, and he knew how to use it to his advantage.

He had pumped at a slow pace. Then he pounds a little differently inside of Ciara's body. Ciara grabbed his back and placed her hands on his shoulders. Each pound made her moan.

"I got it, daddy."

"You got it!"

"Oh yes. I love this dick! Don't stop, please! Don't stop!" said Ciara

Xavier looked at her, then kissed her, stroking her in just the right spots, and began to feel numb.

"So amazing! Oh my god, Xavier! Xavier!" she yelled

Xavier pumped again and again until they climaxed simultaneously.

"I don't want to pull out. This feels too fucking good," said Xavier

"Cum in me, Xavier."

She grabbed him tighter. He didn't try to let her go, and he ejaculated inside of her

Then he whispered in her ear, "I love you."

One tear fell from her eyes. As she said, "I love you too."

Then he got up a little and sat on the couch where they both sat back and reflected. Ciara couldn't even move. He fell asleep instantly.

Meanwhile, Cecilia was about to go on her break. She figured she could call Xavier.

Cecilia made a call to Xavier, and the voicemail came on. So she checked the time. It was midnight.

Damn, he is not answering the phone. It is midnight. He usually calls me around this time. Maybe he didn't hear me. I guess I will call again.

Cecilia decided to call again. Ciara heard the phone ring. She got up off the sofa. She checked to see if Xavier was sleeping, and he was. The phone was ringing from his Pajama pant's

"Who and the hell would be calling him this late?" she was wondering

She dug in his pants, and she saw the cell phone. The caller ID had said CeCe. She stops the phone from ringing instantly and sent her to voicemail.

Ciara felt hurt and betrayed. She walked over to her coat. The number that was in Xavier's phone is in Ciara's phone now. She put her phone on the table. She decided to go upstairs, and she took his phone with her.

Ciara went into the bathroom. She decided to call the number back.

"Hey Xavier, I hope I didn't catch you sleeping or anything, but I was just calling you when I had my break," said Cecilia

"This isn't Xavier. It's CeCe. This the number one CeCe." said Ciara

"I'm lost. Why are you calling me? Where is Xavier ?" said Cecilia

"Listen, is there anything going on between you and Xavier. My name is Ciara, and I am his baby mother, and I'm coming to you as a woman."

"No, we are just friends. He lives around my way. He is my neighbor."

"Ok. I was just wondering."

"I have a question. Is Xavier your man?" asked Cecilia

"No, he is not"

"Ok, well, I'm going to hang up this phone. I am at work. I work overnight. If you have any questions next time, ask Xavier."

Cecilia ended the phone call. She was feeling so disgusted with the whole conversation.

That was the dumbest phone call I ever received. I can't believe I entertained that conversation. I should have hung up on this female as soon as she spoke.

I mean the nerve of this woman. It's not even her, dude. They must have just finished having sex, and now she in her feelings or wants me to know.

I am not trying to be in no baby mamma drama. Especially from some dirty dick nigga. Now, I am fucking pissed off. I cannot believe this shit. They both got me fucked up. See, you can't even chill at work. I only have myself to blame. It ain't like he did not tell me about her. However, why the fuck is she calling me.

Ciara deleted the number showing that she called Cecilia. She walked into his bedroom and took a blanket off the bed. She walked downstairs, and she put the phone back into his pants. Xavier began to wake up.

"Go back to sleep. I was putting the blanket on you," said Ciara with a smile

"Naw, let's go upstairs," said Xavier

"Ok," said Ciara

Ciara took a deep breath because she had almost got caught going through his phone. At the same time, she didn't care. She figured she owned him.

Cecilia was at work trying to concentrate. Then she remembers something more critical than Xavier. The thought of her needing money and remembering why working is more severe than worrying a man. Cecilia loved her money. She still wanted to go to the movies to see the "Pac" movie.

The next day Cecilia was getting off work. She went home and went straight to bed.

Xavier did not know Ciara had called Cecilia. He thought everything was okay. Saturday was a big day for Xavier. He wanted to romance Cecilia to make her feel good.

He called Cecilia, but she was not answering the phone. She was asleep; nothing could wake her up. He had called her about six times.

Cecilia's alarm went off at 7:00 p.m. She got up slowly, so she didn't get a headache like she usually does.

Cecilia went into the bathroom to set the water in the shower. When she got out of the shower, she had noticed the time. The time was now 7:45 p.m. She had to hurry up and put on her work clothes. She had no time to do her hair. So she threw it in a ponytail. She rushed out of the house and still miss the bus. She didn't have enough money to call her a uber. So she knew she was about to be late for work.

She grabbed her phone out of her pocket. She saw Xavier had called her earlier that day. She wanted to call him back. Cecilia wasn't sure if and when the calls might be Ciara. Cecilia decided to call her job and let them know she would be late.

Suddenly she saw Xavier coming outside walking with his son.

"CeCe!" he shouted

"Hey, yeah, what's up. I was thinking about you," said Cecilia

"Oh really," said Xavier

"Yeah, I have to go to work. I'm running late, and I was debating on calling you for a ride," said Cecilia

"Why didn't you call me or text me? I could have given you a ride if you needed to go to work," said Xavier

"I don't know if you know, but last night I called you back on my break, and your baby mom answered the phone," said Cecilia

Xavier looked concerned and puzzled. He didn't know what to say. Ciara always went through his phone to annoy him. It made him curious about the words on the phone. Ciara is constantly trying to stop him from being with other women. He wanted to be left alone. The unprotected sex with her would get him excited. He still loves her.

His emotions with Ciara were so confusing he didn't know what to do with her at times. He would always give her a relationship if she wanted one. They had a history together. He just knew that being faithful was something neither one of them could do.

"Hey, listen, I'm going to give you a ride to work. If you want. We can talk about that on the way to your job." said Xavier

"OK. Sure I will take the ride, Xavier. Remember I told you my job is far though." said Cecilia

"I got you. Let me take my son in the house," said Xavier

"Okay," said Cecilia

Xavier started walking back around the corner towards his house.

I hope this is a good idea. I don't want any drama. I want to get to work, and everything is perfect. I remember when his baby mom called me. Shit, I don't want to be her. Some of these guys and females are for everybody. It seems as though you can't take anyone seriously anymore. When he comes back, I'm asking him again about this situation. Fuck that. I do not want to be on some wondering if I got to look over my shoulder-type shit. This guy is going to tell me something.

Xavier unlocked his door. He saw one of his sons was sitting on the sofa.

"Hey, I will be right back. You better not be up all night! Y'all got school tomorrow."

"Alright, dad."

Rondelle had company, and Xavier didn't know it. He made sure his dad was out of the house. He told his girlfriend Rochelle to wait in the basement.

Cecilia started looking around the corner to see if she saw him. Two busses had gone past her. She was wondering if she made the right decision to wait for him or not.

Xavier started walking around the corner.

"CeCe, you ready. Come on, my car right here!"

"I was beginning to think you were not coming. I miss like two busses already," as Cecilia smiled at him

Xavier looked at her and smiled. He opened the car locks using a remote for his car. Cecilia walked over to open her door, and Xavier opens his door. He sat down then started the car.

"Type in your job address into the GPS."

Cecilia typed the job's address into the GPS. Then she gave it back to Xavier, and he got the car started.

"Xavier, I don't appreciate your baby mom calling me last night. You know that was some disrespectful shit. She asked me what we were. I told her we were neighbors. I mean, I am not lying about it. But what's going on with y'all? She called me at work."

"Okay, remember I told you I'm still fucking my baby mom. You know I never lied to you. Ciara still wants to be in a relationship. I want to be free. I told her that. She can't handle it."

"I know my thing is why keep fucking her if you know she got feelings like that."

"Come on, and you are not slow. Sometimes you can't control the actions you do."

"She called herself Cece, and you call me that"

"Her name is Ciara, and her nickname is Cece."

"Oh damn, I mean what gives. Why question me? I told her to question you next time. Honestly, I don't like that."

"Listen, this goes way back. When I met Ciara, she wasn't my type. I had met her one day at work. I just left a girl named Tamika. Tamika had five kids, and three of them were my children. She would leave me with the kids. Tamika ran the streets a lot. She was a party girl, always into something. She was older than me, about twenty-five, and I was seventeen," said Xavier

Cecilia was listening, thinking, damn, he must have a thing for older women.

"So basically, you were happy going with an older woman."

"No, this story is deep, so pay attention. So here's the thing. I got tired of Tamika running the streets. I got a job. After a couple of months, I started getting cool with everyone. Somebody told me Ciara likes me. When I saw her, she wasn't what I was used to at all. I'm not saying Ciara is not pretty. She is beautiful. I usually go for a certain look," said Xavier

"Okay, I understand that," said Cecilia

"When she came a little closer, I saw her eyes. Her eyes are what got me. She has the sexiest eyes. You have those eyes too. Your eyes look like a goddess. Your eyes change colors like magic. Almost as if you have a thousand people in your soul." said Xavier as he laughed

"Many guys have told me I have pretty eyes. Now, what you said it's kind of weird. I don't know rather take that as a compliment or laugh because that's weird. Get back to your story, though." said Cecilia as she laughed

"Okay, So I started seeing Ciara taking her out and buying her things. I was falling for her. I started claiming her. Mind you, I still had Tamika. "said Xavier

"Oh shit. The fuck" said Cecilia

"Yeah, so I had to break it off with her. Tamika didn't like that. I had moved out of the house and brought me an apartment. Well, now

I own my house. I took my kids with me. I gained full custody of them. Ciara moved in with me. Everything seems cool, right. Then I fucked up." said Xavier

"What did you do?" said Cecilia

"Ciarra thought I was still fucking Tamika. She kept going through my phone, calling her. Tamika kept lying to her. Tamika was lying, saying she was still fucking me at the time. I started fucking with another girl. Ciara wasn't exciting enough. I was just getting bored with the routine and the arguing and accusing me of shit. I mean, I stop cheating for a while. I got tired, so I started seeing this chick at the job. She found out, and she left me." said Xavier

"What happened to the girl you saw from work?" said Cecilia

"She had me open. This girl was pretty as fuck with a body to match. She was stuck on her baby father. I wasn't having that. I was getting this girl bundles for her hair, taking her out, and doing all types of shit for her. She was a young girl too. She was trying to use me for my money. I wasn't about to let her play me. Fuck out of here." said Xavier

"Yeah, that's smart. So what happened with you and Ciara."

"I'm getting to that part. Ciara and I had an on and off thing. I went back to my other baby mom, Tamika. Then I realized why I left Tamika cause she always was at the club, always lying, pill-popping, getting stupid drunk, and started cheating on me. So I went back to Ciara."

"Okay."

"So Tamika told me she was changing. She had a criminology degree, and she finally was staying out of the streets."

"I mean, at least she got herself back together. Why didn't you work that out?" Said Cecilia

"I mean, it's not that easy when you are in love with two people. So, Ciara came home one day a little early. She heard Tamika and me having sex, and she kicked my bedroom door in. She punched me in my face and grabbed Tamika by her hair, and they just started fighting"

"What type of soap opera shit you on? Damn. Why would you let her have the key if you are going to cheat?"

"Shit, that was her sneaky ass. She never gave me the key back when she was staying with me. Tamika was fighting her asshole naked."

"Oh, okay. I get it. Damn, Tamika was naked," said Cecilia

"After I cheated, she was pissed. She told me she'd forgive me if I get her name tatted on me. So I got her name tattooed on my chest. I mean, she looked out for my kids and her kids at the same time. I never really wanted to hurt her." said Xavier

"My god, you are crazy, though. All that cheating," said Cecilia

"Shit, she cheated too. When s Ciara got her degree in cosmetology, she was seeing the instructor. My name tatted on her too. She likes going through my phone, though, since the incident with my other baby mom." said Xavier

"Sounds like y'all made for each other," said Cecilia as she looked at him

"The thing is, she thinks I will always take her back. I'm not doing it this time. I remember another girl had me open. This girl was crazy, and she kept her house dirty. The kids were running around disrespecting her. She was trying to make me be a father to her kids. She kept lying and getting caught in her lies. So I ended that shit."

"I never understood how a guy can call a female dirty but still be fucking her."

"I know why if the chick giving good head, and a freak in the bed," said Xavier

Cecilia started wondering if she should still see him or not. She didn't know what she was supposed to do. They were only friends, but, She hasn't been out in a long time. The movie would make her feel a little better.

"Hey, I'm telling you this cause I thought you should know. I don't want to keep any secrets from you. I need a friend right now. They hard to get from some girls when they get a little part of me they start tripping."

"I mean, I guess. It sounds like you have a lot of playing in you, though," said Cecilia

"I do, But that last chick wanted me to do for her kids. Yo, I was sleeping in her bed one day and a mouse came into the bed with me. When I got up to see what was crawling on me, the shit didn't move. You can't say I suppose to stay around for that. I never knew she was dirty like that." said Xavier with a chuckled

"Guys, crack me up. It had to be something else she did to turn you off besides her house being dirty.

"I'm honest with it, though. I'm a ho. I am not trying to be anybody man right now. That's why I am not trying to be with Ciara. I don't want to be tied down." said Xavier

"I get it. I understand I need a friend too. I want a connection with one, though. That's a little different. I want somebody real. I don't want a commitment right now. I don't see me there. I have been through a lot. I need to make sure my life is good before being with a man. No man wants a fragile woman." Said Cecilia

"She always going through my phone because she wants to see what these women have that draws me to them."

"Someone is going to get hurt one day, Xavier. It would be best if you were careful. It's nothing like a woman's scorn. I mean, you say you don't want to hurt anyone. Don't you realize you are still somehow leading them on?"

Cecilia started looking around outside of the window. She saw that they were almost pulling up in front of the nursing home.

"I am going to pick you up in the morning," said Xavier

"Really," said Cecilia

"Yeah, I said I would. Listen, here is twenty dollars to get you something to eat for tonight. I don't work tomorrow, so I got you. I'm going to pick you up, and we're going to have breakfast." said Xavier

"Thanks for the ride. I appreciate it, and I'm on time. I don't have to clock in until 11 p.m, and it's only 9:45 p.m. I have a lot of time." said Cecilia

"It's cool. I can stay here a little while with you."

"No, I'm good. You go home. I will see you around the way."

"Alright !"

"Wait, let me give you a hug," said Cecilia

Xavier put the car in park. Cecilia reached over and hugged her. Then she kissed him on the cheek and looked at his reaction.

He smiled at her, and then he unlocked the car doors so she gets out of the car.

Camila was standing outside smoking a cigarette.

"Ohh, look at you coming out of Mercedes Benz. Oh shit!" said Camila

"Girl...yes!" said Cecilia, full of excitement

Xavier looked at her talking to her coworker. He knew his charm would make her forget about everything that happens. The car started, and Xavier drove away from the parking lot. He decided to call Ciara. He activated his phone in his car. Ciara picked up the phone on the first ring

Xavier was frustrated that Ciara did not want to move on. It was a pain to see her hurt.

He knows he cannot offer her what she wants. Ciara is pushy, demanding, and controlling.

He didn't appreciate Ciara calling Cecilia. He was starting to like Cecilia

Ciara picked up the phone on the second ring.

"Hey honey, I was just about to call you," said Ciara

"Why did you call my neighbor?" asked Xavier

"Damn, well, hi to you too. I wanted to know what was going on between y'all," said Ciara

"Nothing is going on between her and me. We are just friends. She cool, and she's an old head. Don't be calling her! That's not cool. You and I are friends, Ciara," said Xavier

"Alright, I'm just checking. I mean, I know we are not together. I am just trying to watch who you have around our son," said Ciara

"You know what you were doing, Ciara. It wasn't about our son. You know he is good. This just about you trying to take control. I told you, Ciara, you and I are better off as friends. We can't be together. We both cheated on each other it's not healthy for the kids. Damn it, Ciara, I am trying to do the right thing.

I am trying to do this your way, but I love you. Do you know it hurts me to see you with other women? Why do you want to be with them and not me? What am I doing wrong? I want you back said, Ciara

"Man, we tried that. It's like tick for tack. You cheat, then I cheat. It's too much shit out here! We caught something last time, and since both of us were cheating, we brushed it off. You ever think we need a break. I mean, I don't know what's in our future. We need to chill for now." said Xavier

"Ok, Xavier, well, Why do you keep fucking me then? Where are you at now?" she asked, sounding concerned

"I'm chilling. I will be in the house soon. I mean, you allow me to fuck you. So I don't think you should blame me for this. You are a grown-ass woman, and you can tell me no! Are you trying come over?" said Xavier

"I love you, damn it, that's why I do it. Naw, I am going to come over tomorrow. I will probably spin the night," said Ciara

"Alright, Ciara, I love you," said Xavier

"If you love me, you would be with me. I love you too, Xavier. My loving you is not enough," said Ciara, then she hung up

Xavier loved Ciara with all his heart. He was just tired of being the bad guy cheating all the time. The kids would witness the things going on, and Xavier didn't want to keep showing them that way of life. So he was trying to keep it as clean as he could this time.

He wanted to make sure the love would be honest and not fake. He saw himself marrying her one day. He just wanted to make sure he was ready. He was tired of hurting her.

Meanwhile, Cecilia was at work. She had her thoughts all over the place. Dealing with Xavier might become a problem. She thought maybe she could control the situation. After all, it was clear they were going to be friends.

Cecilia and Camila were outside until it was time for work. They both were just sitting on the bench.

"Camila, now you see what I mean. When I tell you, this dude is fine as hell. Look at him just sexy as fuck" said Cecilia with a laugh

"Yeah again, he got you opened, girl. Don't get caught up on this guy!"

"Girl, Bye! I got this! I don't want to fall in love, and I don't want to be nobody girl." as she laughed

"Yeah, he going to get you. Look at you now he got you all smiling," said Camila as she laughed

"Girl, please! Niggas don't get me. I get them," said Cecilia

"Alright, don't say I didn't warn you," said Camila

"I will be fine. I am about to get a couple of things out of here real quick. He gave me money for lunch."

"Damn, that's what's up. Don't let Xavier be flossing his money around you all the time. I mean, you don't want to make bad decisions!"

"I know, girl. I need my hair done. I'm not worried about his ass. Fuck these nigga they for everybody."

"Yeah, some are for everybody, and so are most women but, don't get caught up. "

"I won't."

Cecilia smiled at Camila. She got up from the bench and went inside the cafeteria to get her a few food items.

Camila sat on the bench to call her girlfriend, Shannon. Shannon was Camila's lover. They had been together for five years.

Camila and Shannon have a love-hate relationship. Sometimes they argue, fuss and fight. Then they magically back to loving each other.

Shannon looks like a model. At first, she wasn't ready to tell her family she was bisexual. Shannon didn't want the judgment. Then she realized that it didn't matter what people thought about her. The family had dark secrets too. She also had some people in her family that were gay or either bisexual.

Shannon only had one child named, Shaniah. Shaniah received her name from her dad and mom. Her dad's name is Isiah.

The phone rung three times. Shannon picked up the phones

"Camila, what's up, bae. I was just about to call you. You need me to come up to the job and bring you something to eat. Are you okay?" asked Shannon

"I'm good, boo. I was checking on you. I miss you when I'm at work." said Camila

"Awww. I miss you too. I was getting our kids ready for bed."

"Listen, let's go out for the weekend. Let's go to A.C., get under the water, and watch the waves while the kids play in the sand. We need a little getaway."

"Yeah, we can do that Bae, you the best. I know your daughter has been asking to go to wildwood. Shaniah and I have already gone out a couple of times."

"Alright, cool, I'm going to talk to you later. I have to get ready to clock in for work. "

They both hung up their cell phones with a click of the button.

Camila walked inside the building. She knew she was about to get stressed out.

Xavier was almost at his house when he had realized he wanted to get a couple of beers. He saw a girl standing over at the deli.

He was about to walk over and talk to her, but he changed his mind. He pulled his car over walked inside the deli. The deli had a bullet-proof glass window. Xavier had to speak through the tiny opening of the glass window. He kneeled toward the window. He asked for two beers.

The woman from outside came into the store. She rubbed his arm while he was kneeling. He turned around, and he saw the same woman from outside suddenly in front of him. She smiled at him.

"Hey handsome," said the woman in a soft voice

She appeared to be older than him. She was younger than him.

He looked at her and smiled

"Hey, what's up chocolate," said Xavier

"My name is Keisha. You can call me Keke," said Keisha

Xavier loves the attention he gets from the ladies. He feels like he is famous for all the attention he receives.

"So, what's up? I see you wanted to get my attention," said Xavier

"I think you're kind of sexy. I am always seeing you coming in here. I live around the corner. How about you? she asked

"Oh, I'm not from around here. I live on the other side of you. But what's up, can I get your number. I could call you sometime. If you want." said Xavier

"Hell yeah!" she laughed

Xavier laughed too. He was impressed that she had the heart to grab what she wants. She had on a red romper. He loves how red looks on a chocolate woman. When she smiled, he noticed how pretty she was. That was another turn-on for him.

Keisha wrote her number down on a piece of paper she found in her purse.

"So when am I going to see you again," said Keisha

As she looked into his eyes and smiled.

"Oh, I will let you know. I got your number right," said Xavier

He paid for his beer and grabbed his six-pack of Old English beer. The cashier had placed it in a bag for him. Then he started to walk out of the store.

"Wait! What's your name?" asked Keisha

Xavier turned around to respond

"Oh, my name is Xavier."

"Cool! That name fits you well."

Xavier smiled and walked away.

Keisha walked over to the glass window where the cashier was.

"Can I get a pack of Newports?" asked Keisha

Keisha pulled out her money from out of her pocketbook.

As she pulled out her money, her cell phone was ringing. She gave the cashier the money. She picked up her phone from out of her pocketbook. She thought it was going to be Xavier. It was her girlfriend. She got her cigarettes and answered the phone.

Her girlfriend hung up the phone. So she called her back. Her girlfriend picked up after three rings. Keisha walked out of the store towards her house.

"Hey girl, I was waiting for you at the deli. You never showed up," said Keisha

"Look down the street. I'm on your step." said the girl

"The fuck. Oh wait, I see you right there," said Keisha

Keisha ended her call with her friend, and she walked a little faster to meet up with her girlfriend.

Xavier saw her walk around the corner. He was in his car, and he drove off to his house. He arrived home in fifteen minutes.

When he got home, he decided to text Cecilia.

Xavier: Hey CeCe, how's work

Cecilia: It's going okay

Xavier: Good, you ready for tomorrow so I can pick you up from work

Cecilia: Yes, I can't wait.

Cecilia: Yeah, I'm going to be ready.

Xavier: Alright, we out then ttyl

Cecilia: lol ard ttyl

Cecilia put her phone away. She was happy that Xavier texts her cellphone. Cecilia was smiling from ear to ear at work. She pulled out her earphones and started listening to her music on her cell phone.

Xavier laid on his bed, drank a couple of beers, watched a porno, masturbated for a bit, and then fell asleep.

Cecilia was expecting Xavier to pick her up. She wanted to make sure she got all her work done. Satisfying a man was one of her ideas of supporting them. Things didn't happen as she planned. Sometimes giving a man too much gave little in return. Learning the hard way that everyone cannot be pleased damage her.

Several hours had passed. Xavier had got up from out of his bed. He went to use the bathroom. He notices the time had said 10:00 a.m from his bathroom wall.

Oh shit, I was supposed to pick up that girl. The fuck. I can't believe I overslept. Shit, I am going to have to hear this shit. I am going to have to make it up to her.

Cecilia's phone was on twenty percent. She didn't get a chance to charge her phone. She was tired as hell. She had realized around 8:30 a.m, Xavier wasn't coming. She had called him seven times the phone just kept ringing.

So she got on the bus. She went straight home.

Xavier had notice she called. He tried to call her back. She couldn't hear the phone. Cecilia fell asleep while listening to music from her earphones.

Ciara was at her hair salon. Her shop didn't open until 11:00'oclock in the morning. She wanted to make sure she had everything set up.

She was all excited. The telephone rang at her shop. She didn't know who that could be.

"Cece's Hair Salon, How can I help you?" said Ciara

"Is this Ciara, the owner." said a woman on the phone

"Why yes, it is," said Ciara, thrilled to talk to a new client

"Well, listen here. My name is Shelly. Xavier can ignore my calls all he wants. He can't ignore this baby. You tell him I will see him in nine months or come up with five hundred dollars for this abortion." said the woman

"What? Who is this ?" said Ciara

"I said my name is Shelly. Listen, You tell him it's Shelly he knows me." said the woman with an attitude

The woman hung up the phone before Ciara could ask any questions. Ciara checked her caller ID. The call was from a private caller.

Ciara was frantic. She couldn't believe this woman had the nerve to call her. Who was this mysterious woman? Why did this woman say she is pregnant? More questions were rolling through her head.

So she called Xavier. Xavier didn't answer the phone right away. Ciara called the second time, becoming more frustrated.

This man needs to answer this fucking phone. I can't believe that he got another baby on me after all the years I have been with him.

Xavier finally answered the phone. He thought it might be Cecilia until he looked at his caller ID

"Yo, what's up babe," said Xavier

"Don't fucking baby me! One of your females just called me and told me she is pregnant," said Ciara

"What? She is lying! Who said that?"

"What the fuck? How many bitches are you fucking Xavier?"

"Man, I ain't doing shit. Somebody is playing with you. What's her name? I didn't get anybody pregnant, Ciara. Ask her what my dick looks like?"

"You little lying bitch. She said her name was Shelly. You know her mother fucker don't act dumb. We not even together, and you still want to lie."

"Man, that's Michelle. I got that crazy bitch on the block list. She is lying to you. "

"I don't believe the shit you are saying, Xavier. How did she get my job number? Females don't go through all that trouble over a lie. "

"Calm down, Ciara. First, call her back tell her I'm not giving her shit. Then block her ass."

"I'm not doing shit. The bitch blocked her number when she called. How dare you tell me to call her back. Nigga fuck you. I ain't coming over tonight. I'm pissed off."

Ciara ends the call before Xavier could even respond anymore. She felt so emotional at this point. Ciara felt like Xavier didn't care about anybody but himself. She instantly just started crying. All the years they have been together, there was another kid in the mix of them. Even though she wasn't with him, she felt betrayed.

She tried to focus, but she sat down and cried.

Cecilia finally arrived at her house. She wasn't worried about Xavier calling her or not. Ciara wanted to go home and lay in her bed. She knew her daughter Lyrica wouldn't be in the house for hours.

She tried to go to sleep, but once she hit the bed. It didn't work out that way. The good thing for her is she was off tonight. She didn't have to go in. She got on Facebook for a while, liking posts, commenting, and then she went to sleep.

Xavier decided to call Michelle. He wanted to know why she was calling Ciara. Michelle answered the phone on the first ring.

"Hello," said Michelle

"What the fuck is your problem?" asked Xavier

"Fuck, you mean Xavier, you got me pregnant," said Michelle

"You know I didn't get you pregnant. Why the fuck you call my baby mom? How the hell you know where she works at?"

"I followed you to her shop, and I saw y'all kissing. I remember how you use to kiss me that way. Then, you stop texting and calling me with no explanation. Well, you left a mark nigga."

"You fucking crazy. What the fuck is wrong with you?"

"You did this to me. So if you don't want this baby, then give me the money for the abortion, or I will see you in nine months."

"How do I know your crazy ass pregnant? Wait, didn't you say your tubes were tied"

"If you wouldn't have had me blocked, you would have known. I have sent you messages for a month since I found out. I even sent you pictures of the ultrasound. A woman's tubes can untie."

Xavier wasn't sure now if she was lying. But he knew he didn't want to be around her. There was nothing to like about Michelle. Xavier felt she was too crazy to deal with at times. He enjoyed her sex, but after he had sex with her, he realized she wasn't for him. So, he blocked her, and she was getting annoyed.

Michelle cried every day, wondering what did she do wrong. Xavier had blocked her without even saying any reason why. She was so hurt, but it was nothing she could do. She did not know this was around the times he was trying to work out things with Ciara.

"Look, I will give you the money. Just leave my family and me alone."

"Fuck you, Xavier! I'm going to call her every day until I get my money. You played with the wrong bitch."

Michelle ended the call.

That bitch probably not even pregnant. I will give her this money so she can get out of my life. These women see me with money, a car, a house and want to be with me.

Xavier decided to text Cecilia

Xavier: Yo.

Cecilia's phone was underneath her pillow vibrating. She was asleep, but she heard it enough to respond. So she picked up her phone. She glances up and saw it was Xavier.

Cecilia: Hey, what's up with you

Xavier: Yeah, I want to apologize for this morning. I had a couple of drinks last night. I couldn't get it up

Cecilia: Oh, it's cool. I figured something came up

Xavier: Cool, are you ready for tonight.

Cecilia: Yeah

Xavier: lol, ard you said you drink right.

Cecilia: Yeah, I do

Xavier: Ard, I am going to get you a bottle and drop it past the house wyd though

41

Cecilia: I had laid down for a minute

Xavier: Ard, listen, go back to bed. I'm going to get a bottle and bring it by for you a little later.

Cecilia: I don't know what to wear. I haven't been on a date in ages.

Xavier: lol. Just wear a summer dress or something. Just don't wear red. I go crazy when I see red. It just does something to me.

Cecilia: I don't have anything red yet.

Xavier: Cool, be comfortable at whatever you wear. I will holla at you later.

Cecilia: Ok

Cecilia put her phone down smiled for a little bit. Then she laid right back down. She was too tired to do anything.

Xavier got in his car, drove to the wine and spirits, and picked up a bottle of Ciroc Peach.

Later that day, Xavier had called Cecilia, but she didn't answer. So he called her about six times.

Cecilia was sleeping in her bed so hard. She couldn't hear the phone ring even if someone gave out a million dollars to respond to the phone call. She was exhausted.

Xavier called one more time. Cecilia was starting to wake up only because she had to go to the bathroom. She saw Xavier was calling her. She took the phone to the bathroom

She decided to text him instead of talking to him on the phone.

Cecilia: Hey, listen, I just woke up. I am in the bathroom

Xavier: So, you don't want to go now. Don't tell me you are standing me up

Cecilia: Naw, let me wash up real quick.

Xavier: Ard, Cool, text me when you are ready.

Cecilia: Ard.

She places her cell phone on the sink. Cecilia took a nice hot shower and prepared herself to get ready to see him. After she freshens her body up, Cecilia realizes that she didn't have anything to wear. Cecilia didn't want her daughter to know her intentions with Xavier. So, she wore her dress underneath her work clothes. Her daughter didn't like the guys that came to the house. So Cecilia felt the need to hide the fact she was seeing someone new.

Lyrica was downstairs with her friends playing a game from her PlayStation. Cecilia texted Xavier

Cecilia: Hey, I'm ready

Xavier: Cool, I will be there in five minutes. I'm already ready. Meet me on the corner where you met me when you were waiting for the bus.

Cecilia: I will be there. I'm about to walk out right now.

Cecilia got her phone and started walking downstairs.

"Hey mom, Where are you going?" asked Lyrica

"I got a couple of things to do. I will be back," said Cecilia

Cecilia started walking towards the corner where she waited for the bus. She saw a guy peaking from the side of the block. It was Xavier.

She started walking a little faster once she realizes who it was. Xavier used a device, pointed over to his Mercedes Benz, and used his remote to unlock the doors. She walked over to the car and sat in the car. He was clutching on her mini backpack. Xavier got in his car.

"So listen, Are you hungry? Cause the movie doesn't start until ten o'clock. It's like 8:30 right now," said Xavier

"Yeah, we can get some Chinese food or Mcdonalds," said Cecilia

"You haven't done this before, have you," said Xavier with a chuckle

"What you mean?" said Cecilia

"When a guy asks what you want to eat. Say what you want. If he says, that's a little out of my budget, that's when you say Mcdonalds's or somebody. Then you really shouldn't be dealing with those type of dudes." said Xavier

"I mean, what if I want McDonald's," said Cecilia with a smile

"Well, I don't want that. I am not hungry. I want to make you feel special. I need you to know you are worth more than some Mcdonald's or a Chinese store," said Xavier

Cecilia looked at him and smiled.

"Okay, let us go to Buffalo Wild Wings," said Cecilia

"Alright, that's cool. I got to shake my head on that," said Xavier

Xavier put the restaurant in his GPS. It brought up the locations nearest to them. Then he proceeded to drive.

Cecilia took off her backpack. She started undressing in the car. She took her work uniform off and placed it in her backpack. She took her shoes off and switched them from the shoes she had in her bag

"I'm sorry you think I'm crazy, probably."

"Naw, I don't think that. I think you are down to earth. I think you know your worth but scared to show it."

"I didn't know what to wear. I didn't want my daughter to know I was going on a date. She would have had me take longer on what to wear. She doesn't like any of the guys I picked. So I do know my worth. That's why I do not want to just jump into a relationship with men. You see, I want a man who knows their worth as well. I meet insecure men that get jealous because men love my body, my eyes, and the fact I have my own." said Cecilia as she smiled.

"You do look nice. I think that's why I am so attracted to you. It's hard to find a woman who is not insecure, does not complain about dumb shit, but most importantly, knows their worth. When we say, we don't' want a chick who is that easy most of us are talking about women that know their worth. Most of us do not want a girl who is just going to do whatever we say because we look good or fuck good. Now, I will speak for myself and myself only I want no doormats. Said, Xavier

I want to hug you. I want to give you one standing up. I like how you wrap your arms around me." Said Cecilia

"Alright, I'm going to pull over. So I can give you that hug you want."

Xavier was looking for an excellent spot to park and get a hug from Cecilia. When he found a place, he parked the car.

They both got out of the car at the same time. They both walked over to the front of the vehicle. Xavier hugged her.

A warm, tingling feeling went through her body.

"Let me look at you real quick. "

Xavier saw she had on a black sundress and her hair was in an upstyle ponytail. Cecilia's eyes were glowing like a goddess. She had the biggest smile on her face. She felt like a little girl fresh out of high school.

He couldn't believe how good she looked. He notices her curves. He looked at her and saw she was well put together.

"What?" asked Cecilia with a smile

"I can't believe how sexy you look, girl. Come on, let's get back in the car!" said Xavier

Xavier grabbed himself through his clothes, trying to calm himself down.

So, they got back in the car headed for the restaurant. She was smiling from ear to ear. She was happy to be outside. You could pretty much tell she hasn't been out in years.

When they arrived at the restaurant, she was extremely nervous. Although Xavier told her she looks nice. She was wondering what everyone else thought of her.

They sat at the bar.

"I have never been here before. "

He looked around, saw all the televisions, and noticed how packed it was in there.

"Oh yeah, I like it here. I sometimes come here by myself," said Cecilia

Xavier nodded his head in agreement. The bartender came over and asked them did they want to place an order.

Cecilia already knew what she wanted because she always comes there to eat.

"Yeah, let me get them famous wings," said Cecilia with a smile

"How's the food here, CeCe ?"

"Pretty good I cannot complain off none of their food."

Xavier looked at the menu that was in front of him. He notices they had a house sampler. The house sampler had onion rings, mozzarella sticks, boneless wings, and nachos. So, he ordered it.

"What kind of sauce would you like? We have Parmesan garlic and Barbeque." said the Bartender

"Give me barbeque."

"Damn, I knew you were hungry trying to fraud."

"Yeah, the smell kicks in like an old grandmom in the kitchen," he said with a chuckled

Cecilia laughed a little too.

"You want a drink. Get whatever you want," said Xavier

"What! fuck it, let me get a Long Ice Tea," said Cecilia with excitement

Xavier started laughing

"Yeah, let me get one too," said Xavier

So while they were waiting, Cecilia and Xavier started talking. Finally, about twenty minutes had passed their food had arrived. The display of both their food was looking good.

They both were enjoying their drinks and their food.

"Thank you so much for getting me out of the house. I love this. I feel great." said Cecilia

"There is more where that came from, baby. I am going to take you to more places you have never been."

"Wow!"

Cecilia was getting excited, and she was anticipating seeing what else he had to offer her. Xavier started looking at the time. He wanted to make sure they make it to the movies.

Xavier couldn't eat all of his food, and neither could Cecilia. They were starting to get ready to leave. Cecilia had to use the bathroom.

"Hey, I can meet you in the car Xavier."

"Alright, I can do that."

Xavier pulled out money for the food they just ordered. Cecilia walked over to the bathroom. She wanted to make sure she was smelling good and looked right. She knew there would be a long mirror in the restroom.

She looked at herself in the mirror, and she was impressed with how she looked.

Damn, I look good. But, I have to be careful with this young boy he a charmer.

Cecilia left out of the bathroom. She saw he wasn't in the restaurant anymore and she walked outside.

He flashes his headlights so she can know where he was parked. She walked over to the car, opened the door, and got inside the vehicle.

"The food was great," said Cecilia

"It was alright," said Xavier

"Well, you only got that sampler. There are other things to eat here," said Cecilia

"True, listen, I have a bottle of Ciroc Peach in the back seat. I got us some cups back there too," said Xavier

"Oh damn," said Cecilia

Cecilia turned around and got the two cups and the bottle of Ciroc. She poured his glass and then hers. They both took a sip of the liquor.

"I ain't going to drink too much cause I have to drive us. You can have as much as you want," said Xavier

Xavier started the car. He placed his cup in the cup carrier. Then they headed for the movie theater. They arrived at the movie theater in twenty minutes. They just made it. The movie was about to start. He purchased the tickets.

They found their seats and sat down to watch the movie. The last preview was going off, and the film was starting. It was an enormous amount of people in the theater.

Ciara was at home thinking. She didn't know what to do with Xavier. Her head was all over the place. She knew she was not about to be in the house stressing. She got herself dressed. She walked over to her girlfriend's house.

When she got to her house, she noticed it was other girls over there. Her girlfriend was having some friends around, and they had the bottles on the table. The music was playing. It was Kash doll song called "For Everybody."

Ciara heard the words to the song. She felt like she just went through this on the phone early with another female. The lyrics were getting to her. She was bobbing her head a little to the beat.

Ciara took her seat on the chair in the dining room where everyone else was sitting.

"Did she just say these nigga's for everybody?" asked Ciara

"Yeah, girl. This song is hot. Listen, everyone, this is Ciara. Ciara is my best friend, y'all." said Natasha

Natasha and Ciara met each other from school. Ciara was the quiet girl back then. Now she the life of the party. Natasha knew everything about Xavier.

"Sup everyone!" said Ciara

Ciara walked over to the table and poured her drink. She felt like she needed one after the day she had. Then she smelled the food coming from the kitchen.

Natasha cooked fried chicken, collard greens, devil eggs, baked mac, and cheese and made some homemade cupcakes.

Natasha loved having small gatherings with her friends. Everybody loved to come to her functions. She knew how to throw a party. She knew how to make everyone feel welcomed. The way she cooked it would make a chef second guess his skills.

Ciara walked into the kitchen. She saw a couple of women making their plates. So she grabbed a plastic container and started making her plate. The food looked good enough to eat. After she completed her plate, she walked back into the dining room and sat down.

"Girl, you look good. I love your hair." said one of the women

"Ciara is a hairstylist. She has her shop," said Natasha

"Thank you. Yeah, I did my hair," said Ciara

"That hairstyle is hot. How much do you charge?" said the woman

"I have different prices. I have a business card. You can come by the shop one day. I will give you a ten percent discount." said Ciara

Ciara had her purse sitting next to her. She grabbed her business card from out of her wallet. She gave it to the woman.

"Thank you," said The woman

"You're welcome. What's your name" asked Ciara

"It's Shannon. I need my hair done. I'm sick of this mop head," said Shannon as she laughed

"Oh girl, it ain't that bad," said Ciara

The women started getting into a discussion about men. Then, Natasha's younger brother came downstairs. He just wanted to get a bite to eat. He felt the negative energy and wanted to get his food and run.

"Hey, Tyrone! Look at you getting older and delicious," said Ciara

Tyrone started blushing. He likes Ciara, and she knew it. The ladies in the room just smiled at her.

"Leave my little brother alone."

"He over twenty-one honey. He ain't that little no more," said a woman as she laughed

"I am twenty-five, to be exact. Ciara, when you ready to leave Xavier alone, I can show you a couple of things."

Ciara looked at Tyrone, and she smiled. "Boy, I keep telling you. You don't want this work."

"Y'all nasty get a room," said Natasha

All of a sudden, Ciara's song came on. The song is called Drop down and get your eagle on. So Ciara got up and started dancing. Then Tyrone came over and started dancing with her.

"Oh shit, I see you, Tyrone." Said his sister Natasha

Tyrone started smiling

"She does not know about me, sis," as he laughed.

Since Tyrone had a crush on Ciara, he wanted to show her his dance moves. He knew Ciara could dance.

Meanwhile, Cecilia and Xavier were in the movie theater, cuddled up in the chair. They were holding each other hands.

Cecilia was trying to stay up. However, she works so much that her body became drained.

Time had passed, and the movie was over. Cecilia and Xavier had got up so they can leave the movie theatre. They were waiting for people to walk out of the theater

They finally made it out of there. Xavier grabbed her hand as if they were together for years. Cecilia was just really enjoying her night.

Xavier uses the remote to find his car since it was so crowded. It seemed like every vehicle had looked similar.

The car lights were blinking. He notices the lights and found his car.

When they got in the car, Cecila found the bottle of Ciroc and poured two cups of the liquor. Xavier opened up the sunroof of his car to let some air into the vehicle.

He let her drink up and turned on the radio. Rihanna's song "Wild Thoughts" had come on the radio.

Cecilia was get excited and sipping her liquor. Then, she started singing the song and enjoying the breeze.

"Wild, Wild, Wild thoughts," said Cecilia

Everyone was outside. It was like the night was just suitable for everyone.

Cecilia was dancing a little in the car. Xavier was smiling. He knew she was feeling it, and he loved it.

He had rubbed her thigh a little. He notices she didn't stop. She got up in the chair a little, turned around to show her butt, and started twerking. He got a little excited and started feeling on her butt.

Cecilia turned back around to sit down

"Naw get back up there," said Xavier

"Naw, I'm doing too much," said Cecilia

"Now, look what you did to me," said Xavier

Xavier grabbed her hand so that she could feel his pants. As she touched him, she was getting pissed off. His size was not pleasing her. She took her hand away slowly.

"Oh my bad," said Cecilia

"Naw, you good," said Xavier

They were getting near his house. Xavier was looking for his parking space. He was angry when he found out he couldn't park in front of his door.

Cecilia was intoxicated. Xavier was looking in his pocket for his keys. He opens his car door, and they both got the car. She followed him across the street as they walked over to his house. Once they got in, Cecilia had to use the bathroom.

"Where's the bathroom? I have to go bad," said Cecilia

"It's upstairs on your right," said Xavier

Xavier walked upstairs with her. He showed her the bathroom. Xavier went into the room to light some scented candles. He went through his phone's playlist, turned on his speaker, and played some music from his phone.

Cecilia came out of the bathroom.

"Come in the front room!" yelled Xavier

Cecilia walked into the room. It smelled like scented candles. Then she heard a song by silk. "Meeting in my bedroom."

"Xavier, that's how you feel," said Cecilia

"Yes. Come here, kiss me," said Xavier with a smile

Cecilia walked over to him, and she kissed him on his lips. Xavier started to rub on her body enough to turn her on. He grabbed her by her chin lightly. He proceeded to kiss her back. She allowed his warm tongue to go slowly into her mouth.

Then suddenly, she stopped him.

"Wait! This is too soon," said Cecilia

"Yeah. You are right. It is too soon. Do you want some more of the liquor?" said Xavier

"Yeah," said Cecilia

Xavier realizes he left the liquor in the car. So he went back to the car to grab it. Then he came back into the house.

Cecilia was sitting on the bed. He poured them both some liquor. They both were sipping on their drink. The vibe was feeling so nice. The music was just right

"Do you want to dance?" asked Xavier

"Sure, I will dance with you," said Cecilia

The song that was playing was called "Knocks me off my feet" by Darnell Jones

He grabbed her close so they could dance. He began to sing to her while they were dancing. She was impressed cause he could sing. They were grinding on each other. The chemistry was just going so well.

After the song was over, she sat on the bed.

"I see you can sing a little bit."

"I know a little something. You notice I didn't hit the high notes, though. Lay down on the bed."

Cecilia was a little nervous. He slowly took off her underwear.

"Spread your legs apart."

Cecilia took a deep breath. Xavier's voice was so soothing to her ears. She slowly spread her legs apart as instructed to do.

"Okay.'"

Xavier slowly licked on her clitoris and slurped on it. Cecilia began to moan. The pleasure was just so intense. Then, he started licking every inch of her, including her butt.

One tear came from her eye. He slowly places his penis inside of her. Her eyes felt like they were going to the back of her head. She notices the size was much different than how it felt in the car.

Xavier was giving her slow strokes.

"Lawd No, go harder and faster, please, oh my god."

"I got you," He whispered in her ear

He did what she asked him to do. Then he grabbed her head, and she came so hard it was like an explosion

"Oh shit! Whoo. Who sent you mother fucker" he said

Then they began to kiss. Cecilia told him to lay on his back. She got on her knees, grabbed his penis, and began to suck on him. Then he began to get more excited.

"Damn, I didn't know you were this big. You can't be real."

She felt like she would gag, so she dribbled on the tip and started sucking on him again. Then she climbed on him and just started riding him.

"Damn girl"

He was feeling good. He gripped Cecilia's hair, and he started moving back. He turned her around, and he climbed on top of her in a frog position. He had her bottom up in the air. He pounded harder and faster.

"Oh my fucking God. I can't take it."

"Oh shit" yelled Xavier

Every pound and stroke was incredible to her. Tears were flowing out of her eyes. She couldn't believe this was happening. Then he pulled out and tried to bust on her butt. She turned around so quickly to catch it all.

Xavier made a face as if he was shocked by that move.

"The fuck" said Xavier

Xavier went to the bathroom to get a warm rag. He wiped himself off. Then Xavier rinsed the rag off and came back into the room. He gave her the same rag he uses. Then he looked at his self from his dresser mirror.

"Where the fuck did all that dick come from, Xavier? I didn't feel none of that in the car," said Cecilia

Xavier chuckled a little. He did a little dance.

"Don't judge a book by its cover!" said Xavier as he smiled, showing his teeth.

"Hell no, I won't. But, damn, I was not expecting all that. I wasn't even expecting to have sex with you. You sure know what you are doing."

"I know"

Xavier knew he had a way with the ladies. But, he saw himself as the man.

Cecilia was feeling too good.

"Can I use your shower?"

"Yeah, go ahead," said Xavier

Xavier put on his boxers. Then he walked her to the bathroom. Finally, he set the water temperature for her.

"I need that water to be hot."

Xavier had a shelf in the bathroom with rags and towels. So he gave her a rag.

"Alright, I got you. Here is a rag and a towel for you."

"Thank you."

Cecilia got in the shower. It was too hot. So she adjusted it a little to add some cold water. She let the water hit her entire body. The water felt good. She was enjoying it too much. She didn't

Xavier went into his room. He started cleaning up his room. The sheets were all over the floor, and the bed was soak.

Cecilia felt like she was in a trance. She couldn't believe how great the sex was. Cecilia was feeling relax. After taking her shower and drying off, she came out of the bathroom feeling fresh and alive.

Xavier was sitting on the bed. She walked into the room with the towel wrapped around her body.

"Damn, you were so amazing," said Cecilia

Xavier started blushing as he looked into her eyes.

"You were amazing too," said Xavier

"Thank you," said Cecilia with a smile

Cecilia started getting dress as she bends over to get her clothes. He kneeled over to her to get some more.

"I want some more," said Xavier

He slowly glided himself in her, and he started pounding her. She couldn't believe it was happening all over again. He reached over and grabbed the baby oil, and he started pouring over her butt as he pounds on her.

The pleasure was too intense for her.

Every stroke made her have multiple orgasms.

Xavier grabbed her hair gently, and he pounds deeper inside of her.

"No, grab my neck!" said Cecilia

Xavier grabbed her neck as he pounds a little faster inside of her. Cecilia dug her nails into the sheets and held them.

"Oh shit, I'm about to cum," said Xavier

Tears flowed down her eyes, for the experience was so overwhelming for her. Xavier pulled out and ejaculated all over the rear end.

Cecilia laid on the bed feeling stiff as a board, and she couldn't move. He grabbed the towel she had. He wiped her back off gently.

Xavier walked into the bathroom to wipe himself entirely. Cecilia fell asleep instantly. When Xavier came back from the bathroom, he noticed she was sleeping. So he laid right beside her and fell asleep as well.

Meanwhile, her daughter Lyrica was at home working on the lyrics to her song. She had saved up enough money to make a recording studio in her mothers' basement.

She would invite her friends over so they can collaborate with hooks and verses to different songs

The next day Xavier was downstairs preparing buttermilk pancakes, scrambled eggs with cheese, turkey bacon, and toast.

Xavier started walking up the steps to give her breakfast in bed.

Cecilia was so impressed at the same time she was hoping the food would at least be good. He walked over to her with a tray, and the display of the food was incredible. He even had a plate for himself.

"Good afternoon, sleepyhead. I made us some breakfast."

"Thank you. I am a little hungry."

Xavier handed her the plate of food.

"I know after that workout I gave you," said Xavier

He did a little erotic dance for a second. Then he sat down. They both giggled

Cecilia took a bite of the food, and it was good. She was shocked it was good.

"Oh, my goodness, this food is good," said Cecilia

"Thank you," said Xavier as he blushed

"Damn, I mean your sex is good, you have your own house, nice car, you fine as hell, and you can cook. Where you come from?" said Cecilia

Xavier started laughing.

"Hey, I'm a grinder. I said the same thing about your sexy ass last night."

"That's what's up. It's impressive. The fact you are young with this."

Xavier took a couple of bites of his food, almost finishing up his plate of food.

"Thanks for the food. It's delicious."

"I got you. I like you. I want to see more of you."

"Oh really."

"Yeah, I got you. I'm going to treat you like a queen. I keep telling you. Don't worry about labels. Let's just play and have fun."

"Yo, you don't have no complaints this way. "

Cecilia started to get into deep thought. She was so gone she forgot she was in the room with him. She was still eating her food. He wasn't even responding. He was trying to tell her how much he was enjoying her.

"CeCe, are you there." he laughed

He waved his hand in from of her face. Then he snapped his fingers. She came out of her trance.

"Yo, my bad, I daydream a lot. I'm just into space thinking about money."

Cecilia did not want to let him know she was getting confused about her feelings. She was feeling overwhelmed. Everything was happening so fast and confusing.

"Shit ain't nothing wrong with that."

"Listen, thanks again for the food. I have to leave. I have to get home."

"Oh, that's cool. Am I going to see you again"

Hell yeah, you are going to see me again. Listen, I am going to talk to you later. My birthday is coming up. I'm not feeling that. I'm going to be a year older."

"You'll be fine. What are you doing for your birthday?" Xavier asked

"I'm not doing nothing. I'm tight with my money."

"Oh no, not this year. I got you. I'm going to treat you well on your birthday. Just make sure you stay real. I'm going to take care of you."

"Ok. Thanks," Cecilia said with a smile.

Cecilia fixed her clothes. She puts it on top of his dresser. Then she hugged him. Xavier stood up. He wanted to give her a better hug. He kissed her on her head as he hugs her.

"I don't know what I'm going to do with you, girl."

"Just keep doing what you are doing, Xavier."

They let go of each other, and then she proceeded to walk away. Xavier walked her downstairs. He opened the door.

"Bye, Xavier. I had a nice time with you. I'll never forget this."

"I got you; there's more."

She walked out of his house smiling as if she was on cloud nine. He just knew how to make her happy. Everything was happening so fast for her. She loved it. When she got home, her daughter was downstairs in the basement working on her song.

You can hear the music as she came towards the house door.

Xavier wanted to get something to drink. So he got dressed and went to go to the store. He saw Michelle. She was purchasing a pack of feminine napkins.

"So, we even right, Michelle."

"What you talking about?"

"Those pads in your hand. You don't have any kids, and you live by yourself. I know around the time when you get your period. I know you."

"The fuck this is for my Aunt she from out of town. She was cramping badly. She didn't want to get them, so I got them for her."

"Bullshit! I'm not giving you a dime. You better stop calling my baby mom about that bogus baby you are claiming."

"Oh yeah, well, I will see you in court."

"Good, make sure you tell them about that spot on your pants with your nasty ass."

Michelle looked at her pants. She didn't see a spot on her pants at all

"There is no spot on my pants."

"Right, but why would you check to see if there was something there. You are fucking liar. You are not getting my money bitch. So this is what you are going to do. You are going to stop calling and playing on my baby mom's phone. I am not going to hit you. I don't hit females. If you come near my family, you will regret it. So you better think before you make your next move."

Everyone in the store just looked. Michelle was next in line to purchase her items.

"Mam, do you still want to purchase the items." said the sales clerk.

"Uhm, yes I do," said Michelle

Michelle was upset she didn't know what to do now. Being caught in the act was embarrassing. She knew there was nothing she could do at that point. She was embarrassed. She wanted to get even. Then she thought she would just leave it alone.

Xavier walked away. He went to look for a bottle of orange juice. After he found his orange juice, he purchased it and left the store.

The first thing he did was call Ciara when he got in the house. Ciara did not answer the phone. So he texts her.

Xavier: Bae, I just saw that bitch Michelle. She not pregnant, just like I thought. She was buying some pads from the store.

Ciara: W.T.F

Xavier: Exactly

Ciara: You want me to fuck her up for you.

Xavier: Naw. I'm good. I just wanted to tell you wyd

Ciara: I'm in the house. I'm just chilling.

Xavier: Come over and smoke with me

Ciara: Ard, give me a second. I have to get dressed

Ciara was mad at him still, but she wanted to see him. Xavier had that effect on her. She loved every inch of him.

When she arrived at his house, She had unlocked his door. He was cooking dinner. She loved when he cooked.

"Hmm, that smells good, Xavier. What are you cooking."

"I'm making baked ziti with sausage and ground beef, salad, and homemade garlic bread."

"Damn, that sounds good. I love when you cook."

"I know. It's almost ready. I am waiting on the bread."

"Alright, I'm going to wait in the living room."

Xavier had made a plate for him and Ciara, and he brought it into the dining room. He placed it on the coffee table.

The food looks so good to Ciara. She couldn't wait until she ate it. As she took a bite, she felt like she was in heaven. The food was mouth-watering.

"I got some Ciroc left. Do you want some?"

"Yes, daddy, that would be nice."

Xavier walked upstairs. He got the bottle of Ciroc peach and then came back downstairs.

Ciara was coming out of the kitchen. She had got two cups filled with ice.

"Give me the bottle. I will pour it!"

"I got you."

"Ok"

Ciara was about to grab the bottle. Xavier had poured the bottle of liquor instead of her.

"Drink up!" said Xavier

Ciara took a couple of sips of the liquor as she ate her food. Xavier grabbed the remote for the television and changed the channel.

They sat eating their food and watching a movie.

A couple of days had gone by since Ciarra and Xaiver last chilled together.

Ciara was coming over to the house as usual. They were watching a movie and relaxing. The day seems so peaceful.

All of a sudden, the doorbell had rung. Xavier strolled over to the door.

He looked out the peeped hole. It was the police. Xavier opened the door, and he was shocked.

"Uh, Can I help you?"

"Are you Xavier Williams?" asked the officer

"Yeah. What's up?" asked Xavier, sounding concern

"You are to stay away from Michelle Singelton. She has submitted a restraining order. She said you threatened her life." said the officer

"What the fuck? I didn't threaten anybody. I just told her to stay away from my family."

"Bae, What's wrong?" asked Ciara

"Nothing that girl Michelle said I threatened her."

"Listen, please stay away from her. She says she's pregnant, and you threatened to kill her." said the officer

"This is crazy. I didn't do anything to that bitch, and she not even pregnant."

"Listen, man, explain the situation when you see the judge. It's a court date on there."

"Ok"

"Here, I need you to sign here to say that you have the papers. This is to show that you received them." said the officer

Xavier saw the papers, and he signed them.

He grabbed his copy from the officer, and then the officer walked away. He shut the door, and he was agitated.

"What happened ?" asked Ciara as she sat on the sofa

Xavier walked over to her and sat down.

"Look at this shit!" said Xavier

Ciara looked over the paperwork. It said that Xavier had threatened her in the supermarket in front of several witnesses. He was demanding her to be with him. She stated Xavier stalks her at her job and has been trying to get her fired. She also said he broke her window to get in her house, and she had to pay $1000 to get the window fixed.

"Oh fuck this. What is Michelle's number? I will call her." said Ciara

"Naw, let that bitch breathe. I will have a lawyer for that day. Besides, she will lie and say I got you to scare her as well.," said Xavier

Xavier couldn't finish his food. He was trying to think of something he could do. So, Xavier decided to smoke some weed. He got a bag that had his shorts inside them, and he got a blunt and decided to roll up the weed.

Ciara saw the pain in his face. She kept eating her food, and she watched him roll the weed up. He lit the blunt tip and started smoking it, and then he passed it to her.

Michelle was at home. She needed that money. The woman felt obligated of every drop of cash Xavier had. She kept giving him money, taking him out, buying him clothes, sneakers and shoes. Michelle found out he was making up stories about being broke when he had more money than her. She felt played and betrayed and had confronted him about it. He told her that was crazy. Then he started seeing her cousin, her ex-best friend, neighbors, and she felt more betrayed.

Michelle kept playing all these characters to impress Xavier, but he did not like it. He knew she was lying and not being herself. It turned him off. She always got caught. One time Michelle told him she got beaten up by many women because they did not want to pay their rent. She had him think she owned an apartment building. The whole time Michelle was renting rooms from abandoned houses. Finally, a tenant sued her for not fixing up the property, and she got into serious trouble.

The city found out she was collecting rent from houses she did not even own. However, the houses were abandoned for so long by the original owners. The courts allowed her to keep the homes. Michelle had to provide receipts showing the materials she uses to fix the properties and obtain a license for each home.

Xavier would give Michelle's cousin whatever she needed. He lost all respect for Michelle. She didn't know how she lost him. She loved him and thought if she gets him whatever he wants that would make him happy.

Michelle brought him so much for his birthday. Then, she went on Facebook to show everyone what she purchases for Xavier. The caption was, "This is how you treat your man."

The photo display showed t-shirts, socks, underwear, a pair of sweatsuits, boots, and sneakers.

It didn't help her sending him messages when he didn't want to be bothered. He only called when he wanted sex. Then he would kick her out. She often cried and wondered why did he treat her like that.

So she moved on and started talking to other guys. She wanted him, and it seems like no guy could replace him. Even though he became an asshole, she still craved his sex. He liked her in the beginning. He wanted the best for her. She couldn't see how he felt for her because she told all her business to all her friends. One of her girlfriends secretly had a crush on him. She was giving her bad advice on purpose because she wanted him.

Xavier made up a story so he can get with the woman, and Michelle was furious. She cried every day about it. But, unfortunately, Xavier did not care about her feelings, and he kept sleeping with her friends, cousins, and even her co-workers.

Xavier didn't care about her emotions anymore. Michelle would confess her love to him. He felt like she was getting crazy. No empathy was giving to her at all. Xavier would lie to her and tell her he loved her, so he gets the money to pay his rent, bills and take care of other females. He made more money than she did. Xavier saw this woman did not think highly of herself. He figured he could save money to do whatever he needed to do.

He was using the woman. Xavier even had her friends and cousins in on the scam. Michelle thought if she allowed him to be free, maybe he would settle with her. Michelle believed that she was supposed to please a man, and he would please her in return. She did not understand that it only works if the man loves you too.

Michelle could not focus at work anymore, and the job terminated her. Thoughts of Xavier were on her mind constantly. The pain of him not contacting her was hurtful. Every day Michelle would cry, wishing he would call or see her. It turned him off that she kept chasing him. Xavier would see her messages and just ignore them. So, she would reference money, and then he would call her back. Until one day, he stopped calling her even if she mentioned money.

Meanwhile, Cecilia was at home, just feeling relaxed and at ease. She was at home just reading a book. She was a little tired, but she texts Xavier.

Cecilia: Hey, Xavier, I just wanted to say hi. I can't wait to see what you have planned for my birthday.

Xavier felt his phone vibrate from his pocket. He ignored it. Xavier didn't want Ciara to start tripping on him. He was not in the mood to talk to anyone.

Ciara notices he didn't want to be bothered. Her mood was changing with him. She didn't know what to do for him. She wanted to be there.

"What are you going to do?"

"When I get to court, I will worry about that, Ciara. You know this all because she is bitter right now."

"Something is wrong with her."

"I don't want to talk about her right now. "

"Okay, cool, I understand."

"Naw, you good. I'm not about to have us sit here and be depressed. Get your ass up. We about to go out."

"Where are we going to go? We just ate"

"It's hot. Let's go to A.C. Ciara."

"Oh shit, okay. I'm down. "

"Alright, so get that ass up."

Xavier was making sure he had his money in his pocket. He was trying to forget his stressful moment.

Ciara went upstairs and then came downstairs with two beach towels.

"Damn, I don't have any swim clothes to go to A.C."

"Fuck it. We won't need it, Ciara. We good!"

So Xavier grabbed his wallet and his remote for his car. Then they left for Atlantic City.

Lyrica was writing her poem.

She wanted her mom to hear it. She came running upstairs from the basement.

"Mom.......!" she yelled

Lyrica was so happy she was finally finished

"Lyrica, what's wrong.?" said Cecilia

"I have this poem, mom. You have to hear it. Now it does have cursing in it. So please don't get mad." said Lyrica

"Your good baby. What's the name of your poem?"

"Why did you lead me on?" said Lyrica

Lyrica began to read her poem. It went like this.

Why did you lead me on?

It is the tears that hit you first.

The lies it feels rehearse

I feel like I have been here before

What was I, your whore?

Did you see me as a joke?

I mean, you found it funny to lead me on.

64

You told me you just wanted me

My love for you felt like a fantasy

Now you wonder why I am gone

I wish I can take my heart back

I am trying to stay strong

Why did you lead me on?

Do not tell me I love you

You misguided delusional bitch

You think I am sticking around you are crazy ass bitch

I have felt deep into you

I have memories of you

Screw you and your family because they knew

I did nothing but love you

Now, I see loving you was wrong

Why did you lead me on?

Cecilia started clapping. Lyrica's friends were at the house too, and they started clapping.

"Oh my god, Yes, baby girl, I love this. The poem sounds like a rap song. I like it. I mean, even though you were cursing towards the end of the poem, I felt that shit. I think other people will relate, maybe even some men." said Cecilia

"Yeah, mom, I been practicing all week. I'm going to the show tonight to perform."

"Wait, but I have to work tonight."

"Mom, it's okay. We are going to record it. I'm so excited, mom. We will get out of Philly, and I'm getting us that house you always wanted. "

"I'm proud of you, baby girl."

"Yeah, Ms. Harris, she's good. One day you have to look at one of her shows. She has talent." said Tyrone

Tyrone was Lyrica's boyfriend. They have been seeing each other since her first year of high school.

Tyrone is a knowledgeable man. His mother had him read a lot of the books that were not in schools. She told him to educate himself. She said the school only could provide you with so much. You have to read between the lines and find your answers.

Tyrone and Lyrica are a power couple. They both have dreadlocks and tattoos. Everything they did, they have done it together, and they had taken pictures.

They are in love, and nothing can stop their dreams.

Ciara and Xavier had arrived at Atlantic city in one hour and twenty minutes. Ciara was happy. The breeze felt nice. They were just sitting on the beach. It was packed. So many people from other cities had decided to come there.

"I'm glad we are here. This feels nice," said Ciara

"I know. It's always better to get away from Philly," said Xavier

"Yeah," said Ciara with a smile

Ciara was looking around, enjoying the view. When she noticed a woman staring over at her and Xavier, she tried not to pay it, no mind. She glances over at Xavier to see if he was giving her any eye contact. He wasn't making eye contact with this woman. So she turned back around and paid it no mind

"What's wrong?" Xavier questioned

"Nothing "

She smiled to reassure him it was nothing. She didn't want Xavier to stress out since he was a little happier from leaving the house. She also was delighted cause they haven't been out in a long time. Xavier stopped taking her out because she would always use the kids as an excuse.

"Come on, let's go get our feet wet," said Xavier

Ciara and Xavier got up, holding hands, smiling, looking like they had no care in the world.

Cecilia was at home, all excited with her daughter. When her cell phone had started ringing, she answered the call. It was Camila on the phone

"Hey girl, How are you?"

"Girl, I'm fine. I couldn't be happier. Why what's up?" asked Cecilia

"Nothing, Do you work tonight.?" asked Camila

"Yeah, girl, I do. I didn't get any sleep. I'm going be coming in there tired as hell." said Cecilia

"Listen, How well do you know about your boy Xavier and his baby mother's relationship."

"Oh, they are friends, from what I know. He and I are just friends. We are not serious or official or anything."

"Okay. I was just asking. I don't want to see you hurt, girl."

"Girl, I'm good. He tells me everything about their relationship, so why would I get mad. He said they are just friends."

"He tells you everything, Cecilia. Did he tell you he was going to be in A.C with his baby mother?"

"What? Girl, what are you talking about?"

"I'm in A.C right now. I'm off work tonight. Now I don't know if that's the baby mom, but it looks like that could be his baby mom. They are a little too close. There are no kids with them at all."

"Girl, stop playing."

"I'm not playing. I'm going to take a picture so you can see what I see."

Camila took her phone, and she took a couple of pictures from her phone. Then she sent them to Cecilia.

"I just sent you the pictures. Let me know when you get them"

"Okay, Hold on. Let me check my phone."

Cecilia saw she was getting a new download image from her phone. She opened it up. There he was, it was Xavier with a woman looking overjoyed. Cecilia took a deep breath. Her eyes were nearly in tears. She fixed herself quickly so her daughter couldn't see.

Xavier and Ciara were so busy splashing the water on each other. They didn't even notice Camila taking the pictures.

Cecilia got back on the phone with Camila

"Hey, Camila, I saw it. That's him."

"Ok, so what are you going to do. It doesn't appear like friends to me. They look like they're in love, girl. I think you should let this one go. I love you, girl. I don't want to see you hurt."

"No, I'm good. I'm going to be okay. Xavier told me sometimes that he still has sex with Ciara. How can I get mad if he and I are not even in a committed relationship? "

"Are you sure? I didn't show you this shit to hurt you. You and I both know that when a man tells you something, it's to see how far they can get away with it. I get it. You want companionship. From what I am seeing, he looks like he might go back to his baby mom and try to keep you too."

"No, he told me they cool like that. I mean, and we are friends, so I can't care or let that bother me. I just got to play my part."

"Cecilia, you not a young girl no more. Don't let this man charm you into stupidity. Any man can take you out and give you good sex. Let them make love to your mind and show it in their heart."

"I'm fine, girl. Listen, he's not mine. He makes me happy. I haven't felt this way in years. I'm going to be good. He already told me we are just friends. Let me talk to you later." said Cecilia

"Okay, I will talk to you later. You think about what I said. You don't need that kind of friend. You need someone who is going to give you their heart with no ties to anyone else. What I am trying to say it's okay to be alone." said Camila

"Girl... I know. He and I are just friends. So I have nothing to worry about with Xavier. Have fun in A.C and take pictures. I will talk to you later."

"Okay, Cecilia. I sincerely hope you know what you are doing because sex can make you want more. He is doing so much for you at the moment. What are you going to do when it suddenly stops? Both of you are leading each other on to pain. He is going back to her, and you will become a side chick, and he will have other women. He doesn't sound like he is ready to commit. That is why he's okay with you not wanting a commitment. I will talk to you later. Be safe, girl."

Then she ends the call with Cecilia.

Cecilia was a little embarrassed. She knew Camila was right.

Cecilia did not want to get her feelings involved. After all, she was only looking for a companion. She was headstrong, and Cecila wanted Xavier to be that friend that she needed.

Cecilia went upstairs to her bedroom. She looked on her phone at the pictures. Now, it was clear how happy he looked with her. She felt a little hurt. She already knew he was still seeing her. She just was not prepared for this situation. She was trying to pretend that she did not care. She didn't want Camila to know it was getting to her.

She went on Youtube on her phone. She decided to play "I can't let go" by Mariah Carey. As she played the song, she started thinking about how he made her breakfast in bed and their unforgettable sex when they went to the movies. She felt stuck like she couldn't leave him alone

He was like a magnet drawn to her. She didn't want to believe he had her mind opened. The things he did for her were just too fun and too laid-back. She never had that sensation. At least not in a long time.

I see why he hasn't answered my calls or texts. He was with Ciara. It's a little embarrassing when someone sees the guy you like with someone else. How am I pissed when all I want is an acquaintance? I cannot say he's leading me on. Maybe I am starting to like him and want more.

Xavier is not playing me in this situation. I am still working on myself. I am not going to say anything to Xavier about this. There is no sense in making things complicated. If he were going to be with Ciara in a relationship, he would tell me. I am not about to be no man's side piece.

Cecilia listens to her music on repeat. Her daughter came upstairs after hearing that song on repeat. She walked into her mom's room. She knew whenever her mom played that song; it was because someone broke her heart. Lyrica didn't want the pain her mom would feel afterward.

Lyrica was twelve years old when her dad left her mom for the babysitter. Cecilia would play that song every day. The pain her mom was in made Lyrica cry every day.

"Okay, mom, what we are not going to do is play a song and have it on repeat. What is going on."

Cecilia didn't want her daughter to know she was weak. She wanted her daughter to believe she was strong even if she was not.

"Nothing is going on, girl. I'm going to your show tonight."

Lyrica knew her mother was lying when she stated nothing was wrong. She wanted to let her mom know everything is going to be okay.

"I thought you had to work today."

"I do have to work tonight. I'm going to use my sick day and see my baby girl do her poem."

Lyrica hugged her mom. She was excited, smiling, and feeling grateful.

"I know you're having man problems right now. Here's a song to listen to, mom."

Lyrica went through her phone to go on Youtube."

She searches for Keisha Coles's song. It was a song called "You."

The hook seems catchy to Cecilia. They both started singing the chorus at the same time.

Later that night, they went to the show. The building is noisy and crowded in there. Lyrica memorized her poem, and she got on stage, and the crowd loved it. It was just a celebration for talented individuals to come out. Sometimes a famous person would come.

Xavier and Ciara were having the time of their life. They both kept smiling. Then he grabbed her and gave her a passionate kiss.

Camila saw Xavier kiss Ciara, and from that point on, she was disgusted with him. Her girlfriend Shannon walked over to her with the children. She saw Camila looked a little worried.

"Bae, are you good," said Shannon

"Yeah, I was just worried about a friend, but she said she gonna be alright," said Camila

"Alright, well, come on, let's have some fun, bae."

Shannon and Camila had pulled out their blanket and place it on the sand.

The children grabbed their beach ball and started playing with it.

There was a live band playing music. A lot of children were running around.

"Damn, it feels good out here," said Camila

"I know, right," said Shannon

"Yeah, I notice. Look at their smiles. We needed this, Shannon."

It's been three days since Cecilia didn't text or call Xavier. She figures that he's into his baby mother. Catching any feelings would be bad at this point. She figures it was too early. She didn't want to deal with the drama.

Cecilia decided she wanted to go to the salon and pamper herself. She decided to get her hair, nails, eyebrows, toes, and a new outfit. It was a good feeling. She walked out of the salon pleased and thrilled. She had her new clothes on, and her hair was flawless.

The attention she received when she went outside was endless.

Xavier remembers it was Cecilia's birthday. So he decided to text her.

Xavier: Yo.

Cecilia: Whats's up

Xavier: wya

Cecilia: I'm on my way to the wine and spirits around our way

Xavier: ard I will meet you there.

Cecilia: oh ard

Cecilia had walked to the wine and spirits. She looked around for a bottle to purchase. Today is her birthday, and she wants to celebrate. Then a guy came from behind her and walked over to her. She looked up, and it was Xavier.

"What's up, stranger?" asked Xavier as he smiled

"Oh, hey, Xavier. Yeah, it's only been a couple of days," said Cecilia with a chuckle

"So what you in here getting. You look fine as hell today. I love your hair. You smell so good. You look like a baby," said Xavier

"Today is my birthday. I was about to buy myself this bottle and go home. Since I'm off for the next two days." said Cecilia

"You're all dressed up. No, I got you. Don't buy anything out of here! I told you I was going to hook you up for your birthday. I already remember what today is." said Xavier

"Oh really. I haven't seen or heard from you in a couple of days."

"Well, we here now, right."

"True."

"Alright, we out then. Where do you want to go?"

"Honestly, I don't even know where I want to go. I was planning on chilling at home. I don't like being in the streets."

"Alright, I know where we can go. I got you. What were you about to buy to drink?"

"I was going to buy some Suveka Peach."

"Okay, let's get the bottle, and we are out."

Xavier picked up the bottle, and after he purchases the bottle, they got into his car. Xavier knew she likes the massage chair, so he turned it on

"I have to make a quick stop at the store. I'm going to stop at my house and get two cups of ice."

"Okay, cool."

Xavier stops at his house. He left Cecilia in the car, and he picked up two cups from the kitchen. Xavier filled up the cups with ice from the automatic dispenser on his refrigerator. He grabbed the cups, locked his door, and went outside.

After he unlocked his doors, he slid Cecilia the cup. He placed his cup in the cupholder.

"Hey, you want me to pour you some of this. "

"Naw, you drink up. I'm driving right now. But, I'll get some later."

"Okay, I just thought you might have wanted some since you have two cups. Hey, more for me, though."

Xavier started the car, turned on the radio, and they went for the drive.

Ciara called Xavier, but he ignores her calls. He knew it was her calling by the ringtone. Xavier glances over at Cecilia.

He saw that she was content. That's what he wanted.

Cecilia was enjoying the music, the massage from the car, and her drink.

"I love this car. This massage so good."

"Thank you, you know I'm about to buy myself another house too. I am looking to get at least five houses. I'm tired of working. I want to sit back and let my money pile up."

"Damn, that sounds smart. Houses are a lot of work, though. The tenants not always good."

"Yeah, I know. I'm not going to be no slum lord so that they won't get over on me."

"I guess. It ain't about being a slum lord. Some tenants are nasty as fuck."

"Again, you have to put all that shit on a least. If tenants destroy your property, they don't get shit. They do not get any deposits. I can evict them and let the next person come in."

"Okay, calm down, Xavier. I'm just saying"

"Hey, let me get off of that anyway. It's your birthday and we about to turn up. You are going to like this place too."

"Okay"

Ciara was at work. She was trying to figure out where Xavier could be. Ciara was hoping he wasn't in danger with Michelle. She called him one more time. This time she left a voicemail message.

"Hey, Xavier, when you get this message. Please call me! I'm a little worried about you. "

Ciara ended her call and decided to go on with her daily routine at work.

Xavier had a lot of things on his mind. He did not want Cecilia to worry. It was her birthday, and he wanted her to enjoy herself.

Cecilia saw palm trees and glimmering lights. Then she notices a patio full of chairs and tables. It was a big sign that said, Bahama Breeze. The place was packed and filled with other cars in the parking lot.

"What is this a nightclub?" asked Cecilia

"Girl. I got to get you out more. No, this is a restaurant. You're going to love it here. They always have a live reggae band here."

"Okay."

"I know you never been out that much. We are going to fix that. I am going to take you to a lot of places. You mine. I am going to make you my queen."

"You talk a lot of shit."

"I know, but I can back it up."

Xavier asked to have a seat on the patio. They were seated in fifteen minutes.

He loved this place. Their service was always excellent.

Soon as they sat down, they both looked over the menus. Cecilia notices there was a live band playing reggae music.

"This is nice, Xavier."

"I told you that you would like it. Look over that menu! Get whatever you want, birthday girl."

Cecilia smiled. She was in high spirits.

Nothing could make this night better for her. No guy has ever taken her out like this. She thought it couldn't be just him wanting sex from her. He already got that. She had to stand her ground and not show she was catching feelings.

The waiter came over with two glasses of ice water.

"Hi, my name is Peter. I will be your server for the night. Are you ready to order?"

"Yeah, I want a Henny punch to drink, and let me get some jerk chicken with the rice."

"Okay, and What will you be having, young lady?"

"I want the Ulitmate Pineapple drink, coconut shrimp, with the yellow rice and broccoli."

"Okay, I will be back with ya'll drink, and your food will arrive shortly from another server," said the server

"It's extremely nice in here. The band and this patio scenery. I love it."

The waiter smiled at Cecilia.

"This is her first time being here. So you will have to excuse her. She can't help herself."

Cecilia smiles. She didn't know where to begin with this night. She knew it would be better than sitting at home drinking.

The waiter walked away so that he can get their orders.

"Every time that you look at me, girl, your eyes just light up."

"It's the way you're making me feel. I am just happy. I have never been here. I never even heard of this place. We not even in Philly anymore. Where exactly are we? I'm not complaining. I need to know."

"It's cool we are in Jersey. How long can you stay out?"

"I can stay until the sunrise. I like being around you. At the same, I am not looking for anything. I do not want to be leading you on, and I do not want to hurt myself in return. I also do not want us to start something, and I break up with you. Then I may never see you again."

"I know. I like being around you too, Cecilia. Listen, we do not have to put labels on this situation. We can let it flow and see where it takes us. I get lost around you too. I told you I am still dealing with things with my baby mother. The last day I want to do is lead a woman on to a broken heart. I just keep fucking up. That's why I am trying to stay single."

The waiter came back with their drinks.

Cecilia was looking at her glass. She notices her drink was inside of a pineapple.

"It's like I'm on an island of Jamacia. I don't mean to keep saying this. The restaurant is so nice."

"There's more where that came from."

Cecilia was excited and anticipating what else did he have to offer her. She was trying to fight her feelings as much she could. It was too late. They were starting to show.

Shortly after their drinks came, their food had arrived hot and ready to eat.

Cecilia was speechless by how the food looked and taste.

After they finish eating their food, Xavier had asked Cecilia did she want any dessert or anything. She didn't want any dessert.

The waiter came back again and presented their check. Xavier paid for it with his credit card. He told Cecilia to come on. He had another place for them to go.

Cecilia started taking pictures of them as they left the restaurant. Xavier didn't mind her taking the photos. He was happy because she was happy.

They walked into the parking lot. Cecilia kept repeating how much she was enjoying herself to him. They walked to the car.

He drove her to this hotel. The hotel had a jacuzzi. He could not wait to get her in the room.

Cecilia saw that they were going to the hotel.

"Oh Shit, my cat is in trouble," said Cecilia with a chuckle

"Naw, you good. I'm going to be gentle. It's your birthday. Come on, let's go and bring the bottle." said Xavier

Cecilia picked up the bottle, and they checked into the hotel. When Cecilia walked into the hotel room. She was genuinely impressed. It was like a scene from the movies. She couldn't believe she was in a hotel with all the amenities. Cecilia locked the door behind them.

Xavier pulled out his portable speaker. He linked it up to his phone. Then he played the music from his phone.

Cecilia was walking around in the room with excitement.

"Oh my god, this has a jacuzzi in here, and look at this bed. It looks so comfy," said Cecilia

"Yeah, come on, let's get in the jacuzzi," said Xavier

"Okay," said Cecilia

Xavier set the water for the jacuzzi. They both hopped in the water.

Cecilia stepped her foot into the water. She felt tingles going through her body. Xavier was helping her get into the water. He grabbed the bottle. They both began to drink from the bottle. They were sitting in the water, enjoying every part of the flow.

Xavier began playing some music from his phone. The hotel looks like an apartment. It has a kitchen that includes a stove, a sink, microwave, kitchen cabinets, queen-sized bed, plenty of pillows, a pull-out sofa, a screen television, and a jacuzzi.

He lit a couple of candles. The room was so beautiful. Xavier wanted to give her a night she would never forget.

The night couldn't become anymore perfect. Xavier gave her the ultimate getaway.

Cecilia became quiet and started daydreaming.

"What's wrong? What are you thinking? You are always daydreaming."

"This is just an amazing night, Xavier. You are just too good to be true."

"I know, and it's going to get even better for you. I just want to give you things I can tell your not use to having from a man. I can be the friend you ask for and decide you want to be with me. I need you to understand we would have to be on the same page. So, I need you to relax. We both know what happens when you rush into relationships. Let's get to know each other and enjoy life."

Xavier looked into her eyes. Cecilia started blushing.

"Why are you so shy?"

"I don't know."

"I know you are confused right now. Listen, do not be confused when it comes to us.

Xavier kneeled over and kissed her on the lips. Cecilia kissed him back. He glided his fingers through her hair. Their tongues were interlocking to the point she felt hypnotize. His style of fourplay turned her on.

Cecilia grabbed his penis and started massaging him with her mouth.

Xavier was getting aroused but not the way he wanted. He didn't like how she was sucking his penis.

"Let me show you something. When you suck, my dick, I need you to be sloppy and nasty. I like how you suck it. I just need you to be nasty as shit. Talk to me, suck on this dick as if you own it. Come on, let's take this to the bed."

Cecilia did what he asked. Xavier put them both in a position to receive oral pleasure. The moans started instantaneously between the two of them.

The passion was so intense. Cecilia couldn't believe how good he was feeling to her. Her hair was starting to mess up. She wasn't worried about her hair anymore. She was just concerned about every stroke of his tongue.

Xavier slowly got up off of her, and he took one look at her before he entered her warm body. She was so wet. It was like he dipped his penis into an ocean. Every stroke sounded like he was stirring a pot of mac and cheese.

"Stop! I can't it take it no more."

"Ahn Ahn, you take this dick."

Cecilia moaned a little more. She gently gripped her fingers into his back.

"Okay," she said as she moaned more

"I'm about to cum."

"Cum inside me. You feel so good."

Xavier thought about it for a quick second, and he pulled out. He didn't want to make that mistake.

"Turn around "

Cecilia turned around into a doggie-style position. Xavier went inside her slowly. He grabbed her hair, and she was satisfied. She became dazed and confused. Xavier started going harder and faster inside her.

"Oh......shit...I can't take it anymore. Oh my god ah......." said Cecilia

Xavier pumped a little faster, and then he pulled out. He walked into the bathroom to take a shower. Cecilia walked into the bathroom, and she took a shower with him.

Cecilia felt as if this was the best night she had in years.

Ciarra was still at her shop doing her last client's hair. She had done four people's hair earlier. Since she didn't hear from Xavier, she took more clients. She just assumed he was busy. She wanted to get focused on her money.

Cecilia and Xavier got out of the shower feeling good. As Cecilia was getting dressed, she looked at the time.

"Everything good," said Xavier looking concerned

"Yes, everything is fine. I was thinking about getting back home to my daughter. I don't know if she has her keys."

"Call her "

"Alright yeah, I will do that."

Cecilia pulled out her phone and sat on the bed. Xavier was still getting dressed. Lyrica answered the phone right away.

"Hey, mom."

"Hey, baby girl, I just wanted to know if you had your keys. I'm nowhere near the house."

"Oh really. Where are you at, mom?" said Lyrica sarcastically

"I'm in New Jersey having the time of my life."

"Have fun, mom."

"I will see you soon, baby. I love you."

"I love you too, mom."

They both ended the call, and Cecilia begins to smile. Xavier noticed her smile. He had been happy around her too. It was like it was magic. He felt like he was in a trance around her for the moment.

"I am ready to go home. I know I said I was going to stay with you, Xavier. It's nothing like being home my bed."

"Alright, I figured that. Do you mind if I stop at my place since you and I do not live too far from each other? "

"No, I do not mind."

Xavier and Cecilia started getting their things together. They turned in their hotel keys and headed back to Philadelphia.

Ciara was getting off work.

She wanted to surprise Xavier. She closed up her salon. Then she got in her car and headed for Xavier's house.

Unbeknownst to Xavier, Ciara was on her way to his house.

Ciara didn't go straight to his house. Instead, she stopped to get something to eat from the pizza shop. As Ciara was pulling up to the house, Xavier was pulling up in front of his door. She was getting excited to see him until she saw a female come out of the passenger side.

Ciara's heart became heavy, and tears fell from her eyes instantly. She couldn't believe he did it once again. Xavier told Ciara he would try to work things out with her when they were in Atlantic City. She sat in her car crying. When Ciara and Xavier were in the hotel room, he had proposed to Ciara.

Ciara saw the woman walk away. But, unfortunately, she couldn't make out the words the woman was saying.

"Where are you going? questioned Xavier

"I'm going home. I mean, I had a nice night, but I have to get home. I don't like being in the streets too long." said Cecilia

"Okay, let me drive you home," said Xavier

"Naw, I am good thanks for my b-day though. I will never forget this day," said Cecilia

Cecilia crossed the street to go home.

"Happy birthday!" he yelled

"Thank you," she yelled back.

Ciara only heard Xavier yell Happy birthday. So, she assumes it probably did not mean much.

She didn't see them hug or kiss. The woman looked like a teenager to her. She didn't get upset anymore.

Cecilia was across the street. Ciara checked her face in her car mirror.

Xavier walked over to his house, and he unlocked his door. Xavier closed his door. Ciara grabbed her food, and she walked over to his house.

The keys were in her hand, but because her hands were full. She rang the doorbell.

Xavier ran to the door, thinking it was Cecilia. But, instead, he saw it was Ciara. He hugged her, and as he hugged her, he was looking around outside.

"Well, are you going to let me in?"

"Oh yeah, my bad. I didn't know you were coming"

"Yeah, I wanted to surprise you."

Xavier moved to the side so that Ciarra could walk in the door. Instead, she walked right into the house. He locked the door behind her.

"Yo, I just walked in the house, Ciara. "

Ciara just smiled. She figured that since he was happy to see her, she should not worry about the other woman.

"Hey, Xavier, you wanna go see the Pac movie not tonight but maybe next week or even tomorrow. "

"Naw, I don't want to see that. We can see something else or do something else. I'm not in a movie mood."

"Damn, I swear we never get a chance to go out to eat or to the movies. It's always chilling at home. Shit, I was shocked we went to a.c."

"Listen, don't be like that. Let's get some sleep. We will talk about it tomorrow."

"I guess"

Xavier started walking upstairs to his room. He looked exhausted, but he still wanted to watch a little television. He flipped the channels and fell asleep with the remote in his hand. Ciara fell asleep next to him.

Cecilia was at home. She was tired as well. She couldn't wait to tell Camila what happened. She got her phone so that she could text Camila.

Cecilia: Hey girl, I just had the time of my life

Camila: Girl, what did you do and happy birthday, by the way.

Cecilia: girl Xavier took me to this restaurant. Then we went to this hotel with a jacuzzi. We had some incredible sex. I don't know why but I was relaxed. I was not ready to go home. I had miss Lyrica and wanted to go home

Camila: omg, you had a special b-day.

Cecilia: yes, girl. Everything was perfect between us.

Camila: lol, but you know he still with his baby mom

Cecilia: no, he not. They are separated.

Camila: listen, I love you. I know you had fun on your birthday, but he a fuck boy. he was with his baby mom in a.c like they were in a relationship. He probably got other females too. Just be careful before you could catch something. He sounds like he is full of shit, and you can do better.

Cecilia: I will, girl nothing can go wrong. I keep telling you that I don't want a relationship. I want a companion. I have seen too much. These last couple of days have made me like him, but I am unsure if I want to compete.

Camila: Listen to you. You are falling for him. He is going to hurt you, and I can see it. I wish you could see he is leading you on to something terrible. You are going to be a victim because he's not supposed to take you out. It is supposed to be conversation sex, and you keep it moving.

Cecilia: I cannot be hurt. I'm having the time of my life. Xavier is younger than me. I cannot fall for his trap. I mean, who made the rules that say I cannot enjoy our dates.

Camila: The problem is you deny your feelings. It is okay to go on dates. However, you are going out with only him. He can at anytime call it all off, and you will be alone. So, if you want this to be casual, do not always be available. Now, if he stops everything, you cannot get hurt.

Cecilia: I honestly don't know. What's wrong with letting things flow?

Camila: There's nothing wrong with letting things flow. It is inappropriate to see a man trying to work things out with his baby mother. He could be telling the truth, or he could be lying. I do not know. I know he is leading you on so that you can be on stand-by.

Cecilia: I am going to text you later.

Cecilia stopped texting and put her phone away.

She was feeling too happy and excited about Xavier. But, of course, you couldn't tell her any wrong about Xavier.

The next day Xavier went to work bragging about Cecilia. She was making him happy as well. But, it was something different for him. They both were talking about each other a lot.

Cecilia went to work smiling. She couldn't wait to go to work and show everyone her pictures with them two.

She walked in glowing, showing everyone the pictures in the breakroom. Everyone was happy for her.

Xavier was all on his social media bragging about a new girl he met. He had more plans for them since he knew Cecilia was not used to going out. He planned on making her very happy.

Everything was going great for them. Xavier and Cecilia were talking and texting each other like high school kids.

Cecilia was coming over to his house a lot. They were having sex like rabbits. He would call her over, and she would run over there.

Until one day, she got a call from Ciara while she was at work. Ciara had been going through Xavier's phone for days. She saw Cecilia and Xavier had been talking. She didn't like that one bit.

Cecilia's phone rang. She didn't recognize the number. So, she didn't answer. Then she received a text from the same number.

Ciara: hello ms fraud

Cecilia: excuse me

Ciara: Don't act dumb you know who this is. It's the original Cece

Cecilia: omg, girl, get a life. It's late. Whatever issues you have, check with Xavier

Ciarra: I did. He told me ya'll are just friends, and you were his neighbor. I believe it until I saw ya'll picture and texts message ya'll sending each other

Cecilia: Yo, I'm sick of you texting me and calling me. Tell him don't call me anymore. I'm not dealing with this shit. You know what call my phone. The back and forth shit is getting on my nerves. What is it you want to know?

Ciara: Why so you can keep lying to me like him? You know what I will call you.

Ciara called Cecilia's phone right away.

Cecilia could not wait to answer. She was getting sick of her calling.

"Hello, listen, whatever you want to know, just ask me."

"Well, when I asked you what's up with you and Xavier, you said it was nothing."

"That's true because it wasn't in the beginning."

"Bullshit! I saw you one day coming from his house, and he yelled "Happy birthday" to you. I recognize you now since ya'll send pictures. How old are you?"

"First off, you need to ask Xavier what's going on. He owes you the explanation. Second, he owes you loyalty."

"I asked him, and he said ya'll are just neighbors."

"O.kay, and it wasn't that deep in the beginning. It's still nothing. We not even in a relationship. All we do is talk about you, and I talk about my ex. I met Xavier at the bus stop."

"You know what? You're lying to me just like him. I love him. You are a woman just like me. How can you hurt another female for a guy?"

"What the fuck? I told you everything you wanted to hear. Now, you are trying to make me out as the bad guy. I did not ask to be with Xavier. Instead, Xavier found me.

"No, you told me to call, and I wanted answers. Xavier and I are together, and we are trying to work things out. You are interfering with our relationship."

"Ok, I well told you everything, but do me a favor tell him to lose my number. You cannot blame me for what your man has done to you. So please do not call my phone anymore. Never mind, call to your hands fall off. I am blocking both of you.

Cecilia told Ciara everything about her and Xavier. However, she left the parts out about the sex. So when Ciara heard that he took her to the movies and out to eat, she was upset. All her dreams seem to crumble. She felt lied to and deceived.

"Hold up, please! You know, all the times I asked him to take me out, he never did. I mean, yeah, in the beginning. Now he's always tired."

"Look, I'm only telling you this because women need to stick together. I can tell you must love him."

"I do love him. He proposed to me when we went to Jersey."

"Ok. Then you fight for Xavier. I'm out of it. It's not worth it. I just wanted a friend. I will be damn if I am a side chick. My girlfriend warned me about this shit. I am sorry I have to hang up. I cannot deal with this right now. It is too much." said Cecilia

Cecilia ended the call with Ciara. She walked over to Camila and told her what had happened.

Camila was relieved Cecilia left him alone. She didn't feel like he was any good at all.

The next day she saw Xavier while waiting for the bus. He was looking around and looking kind of nervous. Then, he saw Cecilia near the bus stop. He wanted to confront her for talking to Ciara.

"Yo, what's up."

"Yeah, what's up, Xavier"

"Yeah, you want to talk about Ciara."

"Naw, your bus coming. Plus, me and my homies about to go out."

Xavier was hiding something. Cecilia could tell by the look in his eyes. She wanted to see what it was. Then all of a sudden, Ciara came from around the corner. She wanted to know what was taking Xavier so long to go around the corner.

She remembers Cecilia saying she would see him around there. So she wanted to know if she would catch him around the corner. As Ciara walked around the corner, Xavier was talking to Cecilia. So she walked a little faster until she was in front of them both.

"What's going on, Xavier? What is taking you so long?"

"Hello Ciara "

Xavier was shocked when he saw Cecilia knew that was Ciara

"Wait, so y'all know each other?" said Xavier

"No, she doesn't know me. You were acting funny. So I purposely waited here. Remember I spoke to you on the phone. Your voice sounds familiar. I'm going to say this in front of both of you. I don't go around hurting females."

Xavier was distraught with Cecilia. He didn't know what to say. After Cecilia said what she said, he couldn't trust her.

"Tell her it's over now." Said, Ciara

Xavier did not want to say it. He had developed feelings for Cecilia.

Cecilia did not know how Xavier felt about her.

"It's over," said Xavier

He felt like Ciara forced him to do something he did not want to do. He didn't want to hurt Ciara. He loved her.

Cecilia's bus was coming, and she couldn't miss that one because she would not make it to work. So Ciara and Xavier walked to the house. So soon as they got in the place, they began to argue. The arguing would not stop. Xavier didn't want to hear it.

He took a drive, and he went to get a couple of beers. He decided to sit in the bar. As he sat in the bar, he became intoxicated.

A woman walked over to him and sat next to him. She had on a pair of black and white tights, a black shirt, pretty feet, nails, and her hair was flawless. The scent of her perfume drew him closer to her. She was chocolate with tattoos and piercings. She had a nose ring, a tongue ring, eyebrow piercing, and her teeth were so bright and pretty.

She sat next to him and looked directly at him. Her eyes were amazingly bright and beautiful.

"You don't remember me do you," said the woman

"Naw, you don't look familiar at all," said Xavier

"Remember I gave you my number, but you never called me," said the woman

Xavier was trying to remember where he might have seen her. Plenty of girls always thrown their selves at him. He loved the attention. He felt like a celebrity. He started thinking long and hard. He just could not remember who she was.

"I am trying to recall where we might have met. Unfortunately, I can't think of it."

"Oh my god, it's me, Keisha. I was waiting for my girlfriend the day I met you. You were buying beer. I gave you my phone number. You never called me." said Keisha

"I still don't remember you. But what's up. Who are you here with?" said Xavier

"I'm here with you." She said with a smile.

Xavier had a thing for women that were chocolate with pretty white teeth. The scent of her perfume and her tattoos turned him on.

Xavier smiled at her, and He admired her confidence. He didn't feel like she was that pretty. She had this sex appeal.

Everything about her turned him on instantly. He didn't remember meeting her. At this point, it didn't matter.

"Let me get that number again?"

"Are you sure you are going to call this time?" asked Keisha as she laughed

Xaver smiled at her and chuckled a little

"Yeah, I am going to call you."

As he typed her number in his phone, he noticed he did have her number stored. He just never called it because he was stuck on Cecilia.

"Let me get your number this time, too," she said with a smile

Xavier texts her phone so that she can have his number. They started talking in the bar. The more they talked they realized they had a lot of things in common.

Keisha was doing good for herself. She owns two apartment buildings, and she holds her own. She has two cars and five children. All of her children are girls.

After the day at the bar, Keisha and Xavier got close. They would spend hours on the phone. He forgot about Cecilia.

Unfortunately, for Cecilia getting over Xavier was not that easy. She had been crying every day. Xavier stopped calling her. He didn't text her either. Everything just stopped between them. She put "Silly of me" by Denise Williams on repeat

She would wait at the bus stop crying. She wanted to see Xavier, and at the same time, she tried to fight the feeling. Xavier was furious with her.

One day she saw Xavier in his car texting. She was waiting for the bus, and he was parked not too far from his house.

Cecilia missed him so much and didn't want him to know. Sometimes she would see him and Ciara coming home together. Ciara would wave to her.

One week had passed. Cecilia was missing him too much. She wanted to call him, but she made it clear that it was a mistake.

She was sitting at home watching television. The phone was ringing. Cecilia's phone had not rung in a while. It was a private call. She didn't want to answer the phone.

She decided to answer the phone it was Xavier. She was shocked that he called her.

"Hello," said Cecilia sounding a little hesitant

"Why did you do it?" asked Xavier

"I had to. Why are you calling me private? Did you change your number?" asked Cecilia

"No, I am not changing my number."

"Okay. Did you want to talk or meet up?"

"No, I don't want to meet you. "

Xavier hung up the phone. Cecilia thought that was a little odd. She thought nothing of it. Then she receives another private call. Xavier called her once again

"Hello"

"Yeah, as a matter of fact, I want to see you. Meet me at my house! said, Xavier

"Ok."

Cecilia got dressed quickly. She couldn't wait to see him, and there was no time to do her hair. So she threw on a wig. Cecilia left her house headed to Xavier's house. As she was walking, she saw a man peeking down the street. When she got closer, she noticed it was Xavier. He was wearing pajamas and a pair of men's slippers.

Cecilia was about to go towards his house.

"No, come on, let's get in the car."

They both got in the car. Xavier took her straight to the bar. They sat at the bar, and Xavier gave her a look of disgust.

"What made you do that? I thought you were different."

"I felt her pain. She kept calling me."

The bartender walked over to them.

"What can I get ya'll?" asked the bartender

"I want a long island and get her whatever she wants."

"Yeah, get me a long island ice tea too."

The bartender started preparing their drinks.

"Now back to you. Why would you do that? I mean, you told her everything."

"I told you I felt her pain. I was hurt before as well."

"We all been hurt before that's life. She single, your single, and I am single. We all are single here."

The bartender brought the drinks over. Xavier gave the bartender a twenty, and then he took a sip of his drink.

"Yeah, well, she told me she was trying to work things out with you. She said you proposed to her in Jersey. I have been there before, and women don't stick together as you men do."

"Do you know she cheated on me too? We were talking about marriage. It's not official."

"Yeah, you told me she cheated. She made it quite clear you too were trying to work it out."

"I can't believe you. I am mad at you. You are just like the other girls. You up there worrying about her feelings. You need to worry about yours. You think she has any empathy for your feelings. "

"I am not going to keep dealing with this. I told you why I did it. So I am going home. I mean, you not even single no more. So you are engaged with Ciara. So what the hell do you want with me? I am not a side chick."

Cecilia started to get up out of her seat.

"No, wait, don't go! You don't think I think about you. You don't think I miss you. I think about you all the time. "

Xavier calmed down. He didn't want Cecilia to leave the bar. He was frustrated, and he missed her.

"I am sorry, but I thought it was the best thing to do. I have been missing you too."

"I was going to take you out. I told everybody on my job about you. I am mad at you."

"Damn, I didn't know."

"Yeah, now you know. Drink up! If you want more, I got you. Just let me know. "

They were sitting there drinking, going back and forth. Then Xavier and Cecilia took shots of liquor and started playing music at the jukebox.

Xavier saw that Cecilia was getting a little intoxicated.

"Hey, Let's get out of here, Cecilia."

"Yeah, I am a little hungry, and this bar does not have anything in it."

"It is cool. You can come to my house, and I can cook you something to eat."

They walked out of the bar together. Cecilia fell asleep in the car, and her wig fell off. When they arrived at the house, he had her wig in his hand. Cecilia woke up, and she touched her hair.

She noticed her wig was off, and then Cecilia looked all over the car for her wig. Xavier started laughing. She looked up, seeing he had her wig.

"Are you looking for something?"

"Give me back my wig!"

Xavier held her wig to the sky and started laughing. Cecilia was reaching for her wig, laughing at the same time. Xavier kept moving his hand every time she tried to grab it. He finally gave her the wig.

They both started laughing.

"Why do you wear a wig? You have a lot of hair. I saw it before."

"I was rushing to see you."

Xavier nodded his head. He told her to come into the house. They walked upstairs to his room.

Xavier sat right next to Cecilia. He kneeled over and kissed her.

Then Xavier told her to take off her clothes and turn around and lay on the bed.

Cecilia did just what he asked her to do. Xavier took off his clothes. He walked over to his closet and grabbed the baby oil.

Xavier walked back over to Cecilia, where she laid on the bed. He poured baby oil on her body. When he massaged the oil on her body, she felt hypnotized.

Xavier told her to lay with her knees on the bed and her butt in the air. He slowly guided himself in her with slow deep strokes. Then, his motion changed, and he started going a little faster.

"I'm really mad at you. I was going to take you out," said Xavier

Cecilia just kept moaning and gripping the bed

"You don't think I missed this pussy! Huh! I know you miss this dick."

"Yes....oh yes."

"If my baby mom calls you. You better not say shit."

He was enjoying every stroke and every pound he was giving her.

"I ain't going to say shit."

Xavier kneeled over to hear her as he pounds and put her in more challenging sexual positions. She moaned, and it was turning him on.

"I didn't hear you repeat it. What are you going to do when my baby mom calls you? he whispered in her ear

"I ain't going to say shit," she moaned

"Shit, this pussy feels good. I'm about to bust."

Xavier stroked faster, and he felt himself about to release. He pulled himself out of her. Xavier ejaculated all over her butt. Then he glided himself back inside her gently. They had sex a couple of more times.

"I can't take any more, Xavier."

"Alright, lay down. It is time to go to sleep."

When Xavier and Cecilia woke up through the night, they had sex again.

The next day Xavier looked at Cecilia, and he woke her up.

"I like you, girl. When I'm hitting it, I feel like I am the man. But, girl, I can't stop thinking about you. I'm going to make you my queen. You can't be friends with my baby mom."

"Why did you call me blocked Xavier?

"Man, I don't trust that shit. How do I know you are not friends with my baby mom."

"I'm not doing that. I won't be able to talk to you for a couple of days anyway. The billed is going to be due, and my phone about to get cut off. I don't know how long it's going to last. I promise you I will not talk to your baby mom."

"I will keep calling you until it comes on. You don't talk to my baby mom anymore. I can't be cool with you if you are trying to be friends with my baby mom."

"I told you I am not going to talk to her."

He was trying to reassure her that Ciara meant nothing.

Later that night, Cecilia had gone to work. She wanted to call Xavier, but Cecilia's phone was no longer in service.

She walked over to Camila to use her phone to call Xavier. Xavier was sleeping. He didn't hear the phone ring.

It has now been two weeks since she has heard from Xavier. Cecilia's phone was back on now, and she became happy. She decided to call him, but he didn't answer the phone.

After ten minutes went by, her phone rang. She saw from the caller ID it was Xavier. So she answered the phone fast.

"Hey, Xavier, how you been? How are things with you?"

"First off, this is not Xavier. It is Ciarra. Why the fuck are you calling Xavier? You are a fraud! I trusted you.

"Wait, what? Are you and Xavier back together?"

"Yeah, he and I are back together. I had this conversation with you before. We are getting married. He proposed to me when we went to the beach in New Jersey. I told you that when we last spoke. He told me he has not reached out to you, and I believe him, So, you need to find your own man,

She remembers Camila telling her that she saw them together at the beach. Cecilia was trying to figure out why does it hurt if she wanted to be friends with benefits. Then she realizes it is because she did not want to be with him while claiming someone else. When you are single, it's okay to single things with other people. If you are saying you are in a relationship with someone, there's no need to have another person involved.

Then she started blaming herself for telling her everything. She thought maybe she brought them closer together. Then to add fuel to the fire Ciara text her.

Ciara: What do you want from Xavier? He has a family to take care of, and we are going to get married. Please stop calling him!

Cecilia looked at the text, and she didn't even respond. Tears started flowing down her eyes instantly.

She felt betrayed, used and, crushed. The pain was unbearable. She started thinking Camila was right when she called him a "fuck boy" and said he was full of shit.

I can't believe, as old as I am, that I felt for this shit. Why did it have to be me? What the fuck did I do to deserve this shit? I am sitting here crying over a man who doesn't even love me. I don't know if I even love him. I don't know what to do or what to think. Maybe it is sex that I am in love with or how silly he is. Was I falling in love and didn't know it? Why the fuck am I crying? This shit does not make any sense. I am not a child in high school, and he is not my first love.

Cecilia started playing the songs that she downloaded. She went from playing Ciara's music called I bet, Trina's song called "Here we go again" and then when "Fuck boy" by Trina came on, she thought this song sounds just like that damn Xavier.

Xavier had decided to text Michelle. He had been drinking, and he didn't want to call Cecilia

Michelle was out at a bar drinking herself. She notices that she was receiving a text, and it was from Xavier.

Xavier: Wyd

Michelle: I am at a bar chilling. Why, what's up?

Xavier: Come over, we need to talk.

Michelle knew Xavier did not want to talk. She missed him and was horny after having a couple of shots of liquor in her system.

Michelle: I am in the neighborhood, and I will see you in a minute.

Xavier: Alright, cool

Michelle finished the last sip of her drink. Then she walked over to Xavier's house. There he was, sitting on his porch waiting for her to come in.

Michelle was smiling hard, forgetting everything that they have been going through.

"Come on, let's go inside and sit on the couch. We can watch some television."

So they walked into the house and sat on his couch. Michelle was feeling comfortable and relaxed.

"So, what do you want to talk about?" Michelle questioned

Xavier took his fingers and placed them on her lips.

"I like this dress you have on. It looks nice on you."

"I did not come here for that, Xavier."

"It's cool. I don't want anything, don't worry. I just want to know why you are so mad and you got this restraining order on me. But, girl, you know I am no threat to you?

"I know, Xavier, but you have been ignoring me and treating me like I'm crazy. I do everything for you."

"I am sorry, let me make it up to you. You look so pretty tonight. Can I eat your pussy?

"Shit, you don't have to ask me twice."

Michelle laid down on the couch, lifting her sundress. Xavier helped her take off her underwear as soon as Xavier's tongue touch her vagina. Michelle went crazy but in a relaxing way. The flicker of his tongue was giving her some intense pleasure.

"Fuck me, Xavier."

"Okay, I got you."

Xavier took off his clothes slowly, and he glided himself inside her. He felt the warmth instantly from her. The moistness coming from her body made him cum fast. But then, he knew that he had to pull out.

Once Xavier pulled out of her. He asked her to open her mouth so he could cum inside of her mouth. Michelle swallowed him up. He felt stuck and didn't know what to do.

"Listen, I am sorry for how I was treating you. I was going through some things, and I just wanted to switch things around for a while. I don't want to hurt you. I just saw you were catching feelings. I told you at the beginning that is not what I need right now."

"I don't want nothing from you either."

"Alright, take the charges off me, and I will make sure I spend some time with you. It won't be a lot cause me, and my baby mom is back together. I am telling you, so you don't think I am trying to mislead you or anything."

"I know I been with you while you were with her before. So I give you whatever you remember."

"Listen, I am not trying to be rude. Ciara could be coming home from work any minute. So, I am going need you to leave out the back door."

"No, it's cool, and don't worry. I am going to drop those charges.

A few days had passed. Xavier had to go to court for the restraining order that Michelle had against him.

Xavier had brought his lawyer with him, and Michelle did not have one. She also didn't have a good defense for her case.

She had no proof for the accusations she had against him. As a result, Michelle was unprepared for her court case.

The judge was looking at the documents that were in front of him.

Michelle stood up from her seat. The judge looked at her, not knowing what to expect.

"Mam is everything okay."

"I like to withdraw the charges that I made on Xavier."

"Are you sure that you want to do that?"

"Yes, I am sure that I do not want to press charges."

"Okay, well, this case is dismissed. However, once I close this case, you cannot bring this man back into court. The only way it will be allowed is to have some proof for all the accusations you have made.

Xavier looked around, and he saw Ciara walk into the courtroom. Michelle walked out of the courtroom, and she went straight home.

A couple of months had changed, and Michelle decided she wanted to change her life. She did not want to be a side chick or be used by men again.

Michelle started working out. She was doing good for herself. Michelle found a good job, and her credit was improving. She brought her a car and owned an apartment building. Everything was going well for her. Until one day, she ran into Xavier.

Michelle wanted to take her niece to the movies to see "Coco." Xavier was leaving the film when he saw Michelle. He couldn't believe how different she looked. She looked happy, and the weight she lost looked even better. Michelle looked like a model.

"Michelle, Is that you?" Questioned Xavier

Michelle looked at him and noticed he was not with Ciara. Instead, he was with someone else.

"Yeah, it's me. I guess it's someone else's turn today," said Michelle sarcastically

"Oh, you're trying to play me. Tasha, this is Michelle."

"Hi Tasha, Listen, I am with my niece, and we have to go and enjoy this movie. You all have fun."

Michelle and her niece walked into the theater and had a seat. Then, Xavier and Tasha got into his car.

Tasha and Xavier had been seeing each other for months now. She was a challenge to him. Every time he would try to get her in the bedroom, Tasha declined. However, Xavier loved the chase she was giving him.

Tasha wanted to make him wait for it. But he didn't mind. Finally, he was able to open up to someone. The only problem is he was still engaged to Ciara.

Cecilia started making excuses for not seeing him because she didn't want to interfere with him and Ciara. Unfortunately, Xavier was unaware of the conversation between Ciara and Cecilia.

Cecilia started seeing other people trying to replace Xavier, but she had no luck. The guys she met were too eager to have sex with her. That was a complete turn-off.

Every day she would miss him. She couldn't get herself to call him. Sometimes she would see him driving Ciara and him around with the kids. She didn't know he saw more than just Ciara at this point. Cecilia was just hurt.

Xavier dropped Tasha off at her house. It got to the point where he would leave his kids at her home. She was able to get into his head. They were doing for each other.

Xavier decided to text Michelle. He knew it was a risk. But he wanted to take that chance. She was looking too good.

Xavier: Hey, what's up

Michelle: What the fuck you want, Xavier?

Xavier: Come on, don't be like that. You and I made up, remember.

Michelle: Fuck you! Don't you have to get up to work tomorrow?

Xavier: I'm off. Can you come out later? I can pick you up. We can go out to eat

Michelle: I'm not hungry. I have a car. So what you want, Xavier. Please get to the point?

Xavier: I had a flashback. You look beautiful today. I want to talk have a little conversation

Michelle: We are talking right now, Xavier

Xavier: We can talk in person. Come on, my kids not home

Michelle: SO...I DON'T GIVE A FUCK. YOU FUCK BOY

Xavier: Come on, that's not nice. I didn't call you out of your name. I got a check for you. I see you wrote the words big what you angry at me. Don't be like that!

Michelle: How much money???

Xavier: I will pick you up at ten, and we can talk about it.

Michelle: I said I drive. I will see you at 10 o'clock and have my money ready.

Michelle felt like any means necessary; she was going to get her money from Xavier. After she finishes the movie with her niece, she took her home. Michelle didn't want to wear the same thing from the movies. She made herself look so good. Then she put on this perfume that was intoxicating to any man.

It was about a little after 9:30, and Xavier kept wondering was she on her way. He started texting her, and then he called her.

She arrived at his door in thirty minutes. Xavier looked at her up and down.

He was fascinated with her smile. Despite the feelings she had against him, she was happy to see him. He hugged her. The hug felt warm.

She had missed that feeling.

"Look at you, girl! You look like a meal fuck a snack."

Michelle started laughing.

"I have been working out. So, where's the money you said you were going to give me."

"Damn, you just straight forth with it. Sit down, let's have a drink!"

"Yeah, you can get me a drink."

Xavier walked over to the kitchen and poured him and her drink. After Michelle had a couple of drinks, he knew she would be ready to do whatever he wanted.

"Turn on the music! I need to hear some music, Xavier. "

Xavier picked up his remote for the television. He used the remote to turn to the music station. Then her favorite song came on, "Leave the door open" by Bruno Mars. She asked if she could give him a lapdance. Michelle was feeling it. It was like she needed to get out. She missed Xavier being with her.

"Come here! Let me see what you can do !"

Michelle walked over to him and started dancing. He was getting excited. He started moaning and calling her name out.

"Look what you have done to me! You see my shit getting hard."

"Oh, yes, daddy! I see that big dick. Bring that dick to mommy so I can suck it good for you, daddy!"

Xavier pulled his pants down. Michelle slowly put her mouth on his shaft and started sucking and slurping on his dick. He loved it.

"Damn, I miss how you suck my dick."

"I know"

Michelle was making him feel good. Xavier felt like he was having a seizure. Since Michelle lost so much weight, her body was flexible. He knew he could get Michelle anytime he wanted. Xavier knew she was crazy over him. He wanted some freaky nasty sex. She didn't see a couple of times she could have been with him in a relationship. When she drank too much, it would turn him off. They did everything together in the bedroom. She gave him threesomes with women.

He gave her threesomes with men, orgies, and even into couples.

"What the fuck? Turn around get on your knees. I want some of that ass."

Michelle did not hesitate to get on her knees. She was craving for him. The slightest touch of his hands gave her a tingling sensation.

He was kissing all over her body. Then he told her to turn around again.

"Look at me!" said Xavier

Michelle turned around and looked into his eyes as she sat on the sofa. He looked at her as well. "Can I taste your pussy?"

She took a deep breath anticipating his touch. Then she exhaled as he spread her legs apart and began licking her clitoris slowly. Next, he flickered his tongue a little faster and sucked on her clitoris while squeezing her breast.

Michelle couldn't take it anymore. The pleasure was so good. He started hearing her juices and slid inside her again. He was pounding her as if it was a new woman. Every pound and every stroke made them both excited. Her legs started shaking.

"Oh.....shit," she moaned. She gently rubbed her fingers through Xavier's hair.

"This pussy is so fucking good. Who else you fucking?" said Xavier

She grabbed his back as tight as she could. Then she squirted on him. He was amazed that she did that.

"You want this nut inside you."

"Yes, Xavier"

He pulled out and grabbed Michelle by the head, and he placed his penis inside her mouth. He came so much in her mouth that she started to gag a little.

He passed her a towel that he had nearby.

"Shit" he shouted. He walked upstairs, took a shower, and came downstairs with a towel on.

"Alright, what you about to do."

"Wait, what the fuck"

"You got to go home. Get out!"

"I thought you changed. You still a fuck boy."

"Whatever you got to get out."

"What about my money?"

"What, I look like a trick?"

"I can't believe I fell for this again. I hate you."

"Well, you did now get out."

"This ain't over, Xavier. You are going to pay for this shit. I'm tired of you disrespecting me. So I minded my business, and I stop calling you."

"I mean, what are you going to do? You cannot get the restraining order again. The judge is going to look at you like your crazy."

Ciara heard the yelling from outside. She ran to the house door opening it up with her key.

"What's going on here, Xavier?"

"This crazy bitch came in the house. I don't even know how she got in here."

"You know what. I am out of here. I blame myself, Xavier. You are full of shit. Please do not call my phone because Michelle Singelton does not need you. I am doing better now."

Ciara was angry that this was going on once again.

"Xavier, I did not sign up for this shit. I am leaving. I believe you led this girl on, and you made me think we were getting married.

"Listen, Ciara, I am drunk, and I know how this looks, but nothing happened. You had to have heard all the arguing as you were coming in the door."

"I heard, but it does not explain how she got in the house in the first place."

101

"I was coming out of the shower, Ciara, and I was hearing weird noises coming from downstairs. So I put my clothes on this bitch was here."

"Ciara, you can't possibly believe this motherfucker. He lies, manipulates, and leads women on for his pleasure. Think about it how could I have got into the house. I do not have a key. He let me in the house."

"Xavier, that story does sound crazy," said Ciara

"Ciara, you know this bitch is crazy. She probably came here to try and break us up."

"I do not have to that. I hope Ciara knows about all the bitches you been fucking. What am I talking about this for with you? You two are perfect for each other. I can drop names, and she is going to believe you still. I wish I never met you."

Michelle left out the door, and she became angry that she came over there in the first place. She got in her car and drove off.

In no more than ten minutes, his neighbor knocked on the door.

"Yo, man, it's your neighbor. Yall good. I saw that crazy chick leaving your house just now."

Xavier opened the door.

"I am trying to tell Ciara I did not invite her in the house. I told her to get out. I don't know how that crazy bitch came in here."

Kevin lived next door. He knew all about Michelle because he and Xavier use to have sex with her all the time. Ciara respected Kevin, so he knew she would believe him.

The row home walls were so thin he heard everything that was going on.

"Ciara, that girl crazy." Said, Kevin

Ciara looked at Kevin and Xavier, and she went upstairs.

"Yo, bro, I am glad you were home. Ciara would have believed that crazy chick."

"Yeah, man, see you later.

Kevin went back inside his house, and Xavier shut the door.

Xavier had no care in the world for what he just did to Michelle. He got what he wanted and didn't know she was pissed off this time. He always took her feelings for granted.

The next day Michelle went to the gym.

She had completely lost it. Her mental status was gone entirely. She blamed herself for going back to Xavier.

I should go by a damn dildo. Men only do what you allow them to do. I do not deserve this shit.

Xavier waited until Ciara had gone to work the next day. He texted Michelle again

Xavier: Yo

Michelle ignored the text. She did not like everything that had happened to her last night.

Xavier: Me and you are good. Everything we did need to stop. I am not trying to hurt you. You are catching feelings, and last night was crazy. So, what I am saying is goodbye, Michelle. Our lives must move on, and when a guy tells you to leave, you got to learn to go, girl. I hope you get yourself together. I have to have you out of my life from this day forth. I promise I am not trying to hurt you. I can see that you love me. I told you my girl was on her way, and you snapped at me. You should have just left, and we have never gotten caught.

Michelle felt her phone vibrating in her pocket. When she read the text, she was angrier than ever. It was too much disrespect that Michelle could not handle. So she left the gym and when straight home to drink until she started crying.

Once again, I manage to be a fucking dumbass on this exceptional good dick-having mother fucker. I cannot even say he played me. I played myself, knowing his intentions. I was not bothering him anymore. So why the fuck did he not just leave me alone? Who gives someone good sex and then cuts me off. Talking about you don't want to hurt me. I hate that mother fucker. He's is full of shit. The way he leads a woman on is crazy.

He makes the woman feel good then throws her away like toys. The crazy part his intentions are noticeable, but because his dick is so good, you fall for the dumbshit.

I do know what to do this time. I do not understand why I went to Xavier's house. When he called me, I should have ignored him. But, instead, I gave him the power to use me. He leads all women on, and he does not even respect his fiancé. That's is he is going to get married.

Michelle had no one to talk to about the pain she was having. She was upset because her life was different. Allowing him to come into her life again set a wound. She gained all her weight back and more. Depression was at an all-time high for her.

Xavier had seen several women within that year. He was causing them all pain and grief emotionally.

One day he saw Cecilia waiting for the bus. He remembered how beautiful she looked. So he walked over to her.

"Cece"

She looked at him.

"I miss you so much, Xavier."

"Alright, so why didn't you call me."

"Your baby mom said that you two were getting married. Why would I interfere with that?"

"Girl, I told you, Ciara, and I was not in a relationship. I didn't propose to her until you ghosted me. She just said that to you cause she wants to be with me. I was single. When you did not call me, I just said fuck it. Let me work out my shit with my baby mom and me. Then she started tripping, so I started seeing other people. I was thinking about you."

"No! She called me from your phone. You look good, Xavier. I think about you all the time. But I do not do games."

"Why didn't you call me ?"

"Again...I don't do drama. I repeat. I do not do drama. You have the wrong chick for that."

"Listen, let's start over again what you about to do now."

"I am about to go to the market. I have to get some food."

"Come with me."

"What about Ciara?"

"We are having problems again. So come to daddy and let me take care of you. Let me pamper you real quick. I know we discuss not putting labels on anything but Do you want to see if it will work between us? I mean, not pressure Cecilia. I am feeling you."

"Alright, I mean, I am feeling you too. But, you are showing something different."

"Good. We out" as he laughed

Xavier took Cecilia shopping. He walked into the store, and he saw Ciara's sister. He knew when he saw the sister it would be trouble. Ciara's sister's name was Kayla, and she didn't like Xavier for anything. She wanted Ciara to leave him alone. He was no good for her.

Kayla would see Xavier with other women and tell Ciara. Ciara would break up with him and leave him alone. Then Xavier would call and say he miss her. She would fall for his games, and then he would hurt her again.

Kayla texted Ciara to let her know Xavier is also inside the mall. He told Cecilia to come on and go to another store. Cecilia wasn't ready to go because she saw a couple of outfits she wanted. She saw he tried to leave so she decided to go too.

"Well, where are you going so fast, Xavier."

"Kayla, I'm not in the mood for your shit."

"Come on, Xavier. Don't be like that! So who is the young lady your with."

"This is Cecilia"

"Do she know about my sister?" asked Kayla sarcastically

Cecilia looked at Xavier. She was not in the mood to get into a confrontation.

"Xavier, I'm going to meet you at the other store."

"Yeah, you do that bitch" said Kayla

"Excuse me! I don't have time for this shit. Xavier, I don't do drama. I will be at the store."

"Alright, Cecilia. "I will meet you over there. I have to handle something. Kayla, you don't disrespect Cecilia like that."

Cecilia heard Xavier defend her, so she did not think anything wrong. She was trusting Xavier's words.

"Fuck your friend and fuck your weak ass too. I don't even know what my sister sees in you."

Cecilia walked over to the other store. She didn't turn around because she didn't want to be a part of the argument.

Ciara walked right past Cecilia, not even noticing it was her. However, she did see Xavier talking to her sister.

"What are you doing in here," asked Ciara

"I will tell you what he was doing in here. His little dirty dick ass was buying some bitch some clothes on your birthday."

"No, I wasn't. I was getting you something. The female that was with me was just in the store helping me find you something."

"Xavier, so why was she in the plus-size section and my sister far from being a big girl."

"Yo. Why the fuck are you always trying to start Kayla?"

"Don't talk to my sister like that!"

Cecilia text Xavier and told him that she had an emergency and needed to go home. He thought that was a good thing. It made it a little easier on him. He didn't want to do too much explaining about anything.

"Come on, Ciara, we can talk about this in the car. Unless you brought your car."

"I did bring my car. Kayla, here are my keys. I'm going to get in the car with Xavier. After you finish shopping, you can bring the vehicle to Xavier's house, and I can drive you back home. "

"Alright, sis, I love you and be safe," said Kayla

Xavier and Ciara headed for the parking lot. He saw a couple of his friends, and he was saying hi to them. Ciara decided she wanted to wait in the car because she figured Xavier would talk forever.

Michelle was at the mall, and she was coming out of one of the stores. She saw Xavier outside talking to his friends. She couldn't take his happiness after the way he has treated her.

"Yo Xavier! Come here. I want to talk to you!"

Xavier turned around, and he saw it was Michelle. But, unfortunately, he was not in the mood for her today.

"Yo, I don't have time for this, Michelle. Could you leave me alone? I told you we must move on and go our separate ways. Now don't beg because it's not a good look."

Xavier's friends started laughing at her. Finally, Michelle was tired of being laughed at and being used by all of his friends.

"Fuck, why are you still messing with that crazy chick?" said one of Xavier's friends

"Man, I told her we have to move on. Listen, girl, you not my type. I'm sorry. Go home. We have nothing to discuss," said Xavier

"No, Xavier, it's time I teach your ass a lesson. I'm tired of your shit! You always lead me on. I never wanted to be your girlfriend. I only wanted to be your friend, and you constantly shit on me. My stupid ass was always there for you."

"Fuck out of here with your crazy ass. What the hell you do to yourself? Last year you were looking bad bitch, and now you look like a hot mess."

"No fuck you, You did this to me. How you fuck me real good? Just cut me off like I'm trash. How can you live with yourself, Xavier." Said Michelle as she started to burst into tears.

"Bitch! Nobody wants your nasty ass."

"I wasn't nasty when you were eating my pussy. I have been following you, and you said it was just you and Ciara now. You were mad you got caught that day. Does she know Tasha and those other females you have been seeing? I was doing good, and you were bothering me. As a matter of fact..." she paused

In slow motion, she pulled out her gun. Everyone started running, and Ciara was sitting in the car with the door opened. You could see her legs facing towards Xavier and his friends. Ciara tried rushing her legs back in the car. As she tried closing the door, she got shot, and she screamed instantly.

"Oh my god, I got shot!"

She couldn't believe this had happened to her. Xavier ran over to Ciara. He noticed how much blood was coming off her body. Ciara's dress had blood all over it.

"Damn, you got shot. How?" asked Xavier in shocked

Michelle tried to run to her car and leave the scene. There were cops already in the parking lot.

The cops saw her running. One cop shot her in the leg, and they had to rush her to the hospital.

Xavier droved Ciara to the hospital. It was shocking that this happened.

"Oh my god, I am going to die because of you. I have kids, and I can't leave them."

"No, you are not going to die, baby. I got you."

"Is it true what she said you were seeing all these women"

"Listen, calm down. Please do not ask about that right now! She was lying.

Xavier and Ciara arrived at the hospital.

He didn't go to the emergency room. Instead, he went to the main entrance.

"My baby mother has been shot," he said to a receptionist

The receptionist got on the phone and called the police. The security guard grabbed a wheelchair and rushed Ciara to the emergency room. A nurse saw she was a gunshot victim and took her straight to a room.

"Take off all your clothes!" ordered the nurse

The cops came in the room asking her all sorts of questions. One nurse came in the room taking X-rays. Since she was a victim of a shooting, they took her fingerprints. They wanted to see if she had any priors.

The cop wanted her to release a statement. Unfortunately, she was too shaken up.

"Listen, a girl I use to deal with got pissed off cause I didn't want to be with her. That bullet was meant for me and not my baby mom."

"Would you be willing to testify in court on her behalf?" said the officer

"Yes, I would. Ciara is my fiance, and I love her."

"I am not his fiance no more. I got shot fuck that. I'm not staying around until I die." interrupted Ciara

"We caught up with her in the parking lot," said the officer

"Xavier, I do not want to see you again. Get him out of here!"

"Ciara, you don't mean this."

"Yes, I do. I am tired of your shit. You are full of it. Look at me. I got shot because of you! I have kids."

"This not my fault. Ciara, I can fix this."

"You play mind games with these women. I'm not going to wait around until I'm six feet deep under to realize I should stay the fuck away from you. Now, you get the fuck out of here and leave me alone."

Xavier looked at Ciara, realizing she was in shock. The doctors told him he had to leave. Ciara was crying. The doctors kept trying to calm Ciara down.

The doctors had given Ciara a tetanus shot.

Her blood pressure was going up and dropping at the same time. Ciara was starting to feel dizzy.

They could not find traces of the bullets in her, only the fragments of it. Ciara could not stop moaning from the pain.

Then channel six news came out to the Cheltenham Mall.

"Hi, I'm Carolyn, and I'm on the scene where a woman was shot in the crossfire over a woman's scorn. The suspect was shot while trying to get away. They both are at Einstein Medical Center. Both the suspect and the victim are in stable condition."

Cecilia had caught the bus, unaware of what was going on. When she got home, she saw her daughter was watching the news.

"Mom, guess what happened at the mall?"

"What happened?"

"A woman was shot."

"Tell me your playing I was just at the mall. What mall was it?"

Lyrica saw her mom's bags. She knew her mother was at the mall.

"It was in Cheltenham mall."

"Yo, I was just there. I have to call my homey."

Cecilia called and texted Xavier, and she didn't get a response. Xavier didn't want to talk to anybody. He kept sending her to voicemail.

Ciarra had to get surgery on her arm. Michelle was immediately sent to prison after she being released from the hospital.

The next day the names of the victim and the suspect were on television. They announce Xavier, Ciara, and Michelle's on different channels. It was all over the city what had happened.

Cecilia had a bad feeling that day. She was relieved that she did not stay with Xavier that day. She felt like that could have been her.

Everything that Camila warned her about came to light. First, she had to call Camila to let her know what had happened at the mall.

Camila was sitting home watching a movie when the phone had rung. She checked her cell phone, and she saw it was Cecilia.

"Girl, I have to tell you some shit that just happened at the mall," said Cecilia

"I swear you always have a story to tell," said Camila as she chuckled

"I was with Xavier, and he had told me that he wanted to pursue a relationship with me. So, I was like, okay, we can give it a try."

"Girl, no, he not the one for you."

"He is the wrong one, girl. His baby mom got shot at the mall. That shot could have been me because I was there at the mall with them. Xavier was buying me clothes and was trying to convince me that he was not seeing Ciara. Ciara's sister was in the last store we were in, and she called me all kinds of names for dealing with Xavier."

"I hope you are leaving him alone."

"Girl, yes, I am; apparently, he was seeing someone else, and she shot his baby mother. I wanted to ask him what happened at the mall until I saw the news."

"Wait, he made the news, girl. You better not go back to him. He plays a dangerous game with women's hearts. The baby got shot, and you are right. That could have been you or a worse scenario.

"Girl, I know. I do not want any parts of Xavier."

"Alright, listen, I was watching this movie before you called. Child, this movie is good. I am glad you are alright, but I will have to talk to you later."

A week later, Xavier called Cecilia and even texted her, but she did not answer his texts or even his calls. She did not want to be involved with him anymore.

Ciara called off the wedding, took their sons, and moved down South Carolina. She opened up four hair salons, and she owned two residential apartments. She brought a big house for her and the children. Unfortunately, Xavier never learned his lesson. He kept treating the women the same way.

Cecilia was at the market getting her groceries when she ran into Xavier once again. She didn't want him to notice her. But, he did see her, and he tried to talk to her. He didn't know she knew what happened. Even if she did know he had no care in the world.

"Hey, CeCe! How have you been?"

"I've been good, Xavier, but uhm, I'm off the map. You can't even find me on google."

"Huh. I have been calling you so we can see where our relationship leads too."

"Yeah, You are a little too messy for me. I can't be a part of that."

Cecilia walked away and smiled, showing her pearly white teeth.

Xavier's ego could not handle that. But he didn't show it. He thought she would be back. But, unfortunately, Cecilia didn't care to talk to Xavier or any new guys in her life until she completed her goals for herself. After that day, she never looked back to talk to Xavier. Xavier kept trying, but she didn't budge.

Michelle lost her mind in jail. She would have been out of jail in five years. Unfortunately for her, she was on suicide watch. Once she was released, Michelle had to go to a mental institution. Michelle stayed there for six months and became an advocate for women, teaching them their worth.

She never thought about Xavier and Michelle got married and finally had two children.

Printed in the United States
by Baker & Taylor Publisher Services